AREA WOMAN BLOWS GASKET

Believe Me

Playing House

When She Was Bad

AREA WOMAN BLOWS GASKET

Tales from the Domestic Frontier

PATRICIA PEARSON

VINTAGE CANADA

Published in Canada by Vintage Canada, a division of Random House of Canada
Limited, Toronto, and simultaneously in the United States by Bloomsbury
Publishing, New York and London, distributed by Holtzbrinck Publishers,
in 2005. Distributed by Random House of Canada Limited, Toronto.

Vintage Canada and colophon are registered trademarks of
Random House of Canada Limited.

www.randomhouse.ca

Library and Archives Canada Cataloguing in Publication

Pearson, Patricia, 1964–
Area woman blows gasket: tales from the domestic frontier / Patricia Pearson.

ISBN 0-679-31363-X

1. Mothers—Humour. 2. Married women—Humour. I. Title.

PS8581.E3884A8 2005   C814'.6   C2004-906975-6

Typeset by Palimpsest Book Production Ltd.,
Polmont, Stirlingshire, Scotland

Printed and bound in Canada

2   4   6   8   9   7   5   3   1

CONTENTS

News We Can't Use

Choices We Don't Care to Make

Consolations for the Neurotic Modern Parent

Some Thoughts on Grabbing Wisdom to Go

Efforts at Escape

Preface

The other day, I had to write an op-ed for *USA Today*, which meant that I had to formulate an opinion about something in the news, and this required tracking the news, which is like following an exploding bag of confetti. Facts fly out of media damnably fast, with spectacular aimlessness, and pundits who try to pursue those facts develop something less like wisdom and more like ADD.

"Did you know that the average person swallows five spiders a year?" I asked my husband last night.

"No, I did not," he replied, "and don't tell me you're going to write a column about it."

"Actually, I don't plan to," I said, "because, also, the Middle East is burning down, and some woman sued McDonald's because she burned her mouth on a pickle, and the actor Richard Harris died, and he had cancer, and women who took the Pill in the sixties are more prone to breast cancer, and cancer charities are being given stock options as a new form of donation, and donations are up for Hillary Clinton, and so are polls, and a new poll suggests that more people in Europe are smoking pot, and pots are on sale at Wal-Mart."

"I don't suppose you remembered to buy cat food at the corner store," my husband replied.

"No, I forgot," I said. This is how conversations go in our house—I believe the term is *nonlinear*. "But," I added, "it would help if the dog stopped gobbling the kitten kibble in addition to his own specially formulated Science Diet for Seniors."

Of course, my husband likes to point out that our dog and three cats could subsist quite happily on an undifferentiated blend of sparrow corpses and wood chips, if I would just stop buying into the "science" and "expertise" of the pet food industry. But I cannot. I read the news. How, in good conscience, could I feed them dead birds when a "new study shows" that only *specially formulated Science Diet for Seniors*—or a similar competing brand—will ease digestion in older dogs? How, for that matter, could I, as a worried mother, wife, and woman who wants to reach a ripe old age, ignore what "a new book argues" or what "scientists now believe" about anything?

As I write, a new study shows that "three out of four mothers have no idea what should be in a balanced diet for their children. Food fads and health scares are so common, it has left most mums confused."

Indeed. That is one way to put it. Addled, guilt-ridden, anxious, constantly at cross-purposes trying to keep up—those are other phrases that spring to mind.

But not to worry. If the news proves too vexing, you

have choices. You may choose not to follow it, with the only real consequence being that you never know when the emergency evacuation orders are issued for your town or the cheese you've been feeding your children has been abruptly recalled from the shelves.

Alternatively, you may choose to follow select streams of news, pertaining for instance to global warming, the possibility of abrupt climate change, terrorism, and what's up with Brad and Jennifer. Otherwise, ignore the headlines, and calm yourself down with therapy of some sort. I've tried this. It turns out that there are some challenging choices along that road, too. You find yourself whacking through a thicket of options in terms of retail, pharmaceutical, athletic, vacation, or talk therapy, and then have to select from all the vast bemusing subsets to be found therein. So you might skip therapy. Seek wisdom instead. Dabble in kabbalah and change your name to Esther, hire a pet psychic, have your palm read, audit every single course at the Learning Annex. There are so many contradictory possibilities, you could write a book about it. Certainly, I did.

But first, I confronted a basic choice, an A or B question that I highly recommend your answering: Stand in your kitchen clutching parenting books in one hand and credit card options in the other, while the cats eat the dog's kibble and the phone rings off the hook, and decide whether to laugh or to cry.

NEWS WE CAN'T USE

Hemp Waffles: Betcha Can't Eat Just One

The other day, I bought some organic maple syrup, because I'd read something alarming in the paper about lead being present in ordinary maple syrup. I'm not sure if this was because the sap was being stirred with pencils or because the syrup was simmered in vats covered with heavy X-ray blankets. But all neurotic parents know that lead exposure will either kill their offspring or turn them into violent psychopaths. And it is my job, my calling, my necessity and pleasure, to guide my two children through the shoals of a childhood filled with fast-flowing traffic and pedophiles, pesticide residues, asbestos-lined walls, and lead-infused condiments to a safe footing on the shore of adulthood. So I purchased some organic syrup, and then I went home and poured it onto a pair of Eggo waffles.

After a few bites, I put down my fork and stared at my plate. This is sort of silly, I thought. What health advantage am I pursuing? Surely whatever lurks in ordinary maple syrup couldn't be worse for my family than the unidentified substances that menace our bodies via frozen waffles. If I'm going to be a good mother, I should buy organic waffles.

Thus I went to my local health food store and immediately confronted the domino effect of one organic ingredient demanding another. Organic flax-seed blueberry waffles cry out for organic butter, which in turn demands to be spread on organic bread, or at least on English muffins crafted of spelt, which then require, as logic dictates, a container of organic jam. And so forth and so on, all the way across the food chain, until one has no money left to pay for the children's shoes. Eventually, I drew the line at soybean potpie. People who won't eat organic chicken in a potpie shouldn't eat a potpie; they should eat something else. Like a tofu burger or a chickpea steak. Or really what I am saying—to myself, since I'm talking to myself in the health food store—is that vegetarians ought to get over their weird conceptual attachment to meat and stop eating pretend-meat products. Carnivores don't try to make their meat taste like vegetables, after all. They don't go to rib joints and ask for shredded pork slaw or salads made of giblets.

I also refused to buy vegan lip balm.

"What's vegan about this lip balm?" I asked the proprietor, a handsome Asian man with a slicked-back ponytail and a white T-shirt pulled taut over his muscles.

"No beeswax," he said, which failed to enlighten me.

"What's wrong with beeswax? Is it bad for you, or are the bees being maltreated? They're not free-range bees? Is that it?"

"It's a vegan thing," he said, mysteriously.

And then there was this bottle of tablets for dogs, made of spirulina, whatever that is. The product billed itself as "the natural alternative to eating grass."

"Look here," I said to the proprietor. "Grass is natural— you can't say that it isn't."

He shrugged, indifferent. "Spirulina is probably better for them." Fair enough . . . I guess. But my dog only ever eats grass when he wants to throw up, in which case he could just as easily eat rancid mutton as a ten-dollar bottle of substitute grass. As a matter of fact, my sister's futon-size golden retriever, Biscuit, recently ate a tub of margarine, a container of peanut butter, and a Toblerone chocolate bar, all in the same afternoon, and vomited most commendably for hours. But each to his own technique.

I finally stopped walking around the store in bafflement and focused on the selection of organic waffles for sale. The problem with them, I found, is that every brand on the shelf was not only organic but also milk-, egg-, and wheat-free, and therefore composed entirely of hemp.

I don't understand why wishing to avoid pesticide residue and lead should prompt me to abstain from recognizable food. What's wrong with making waffles with organic milk, organic eggs, and organic wheat?

I wanted to ask the proprietor this, but I was afraid he'd accuse me of badgering him. I bought a pack of Nature's Path Organic Optimum Power Waffles and slipped out of the store.

For the time being, I see myself as being in transition,

or recovery. If anyone peers into my larder and notes the intriguing admixture of Minute Rice, Jell-O, and organic soy risotto, I explain with a vague, embarrassed wave of my hand that my standards of nutrition are changing slowly, bite by bite.

The Doctor Will See You Now, Sir. Sir?
(A Word About Men, Women, and Health News)

I note that a new outreach project is under way in New Hampshire to rope bucking, struggling men in to see their doctors. At least once in a while—for an annual checkup, if nothing else, which sounds like an attempt to address the age-old quandary:

Why do normally bold, forthright men turn into Siamese cats hiding behind the dryer when faced with the prospect of seeing a physician?

In my house, the scenario generally plays out like this:

"Ambrose, your head is falling off."

"Oh, is it?" Cursory glance in the mirror. "Yeah, I guess so."

"Well, don't you think you should go to the doctor?"

"I will, yeah."

Two days later:

"Ambrose, your head remains connected to your neck by one sinew. Did you phone the doctor yet?"

"Uh, no, I was going to, but I had to go to the hardware store to get some widgets to fix that old paint-shaking machine I found in the basement."

"Well, why don't I make an appointment for you?"

"Okay, great."

One week later, addressing husband's fallen-off head on basement floor: "Ambrose, did you go to the doctor this morning?"

"No, I rescheduled. I had to download the B-side of Mike Oldfield's *Tubular Bells*."

"So when are you going to go?"

"Well, either next Thursday, if I can, or probably never."

My husband successfully avoided the dentist for fourteen years until his jaw started exploding with pain, forcing him to go for one visit. I had to drop everything I was doing to drive him—after which he never returned, preferring to grit his teeth rather than treat them. Why does he do this? Because this is the manly thing. Even for men who don't put much stock in their masculinity otherwise, who happily diaper their babies and cook supper and listen attentively to their wives. As soon as their wives say "Go to the doctor," they go deaf and inexplicably morph into James Bond.

In New Hampshire, the project coordinator Chuck Rhoades is bringing men together at their workplaces on the understated theory that men won't go out of their way to visit doctors. He plans five weekly group discussions on health, hoping to eventually elicit their specific, personal concerns. (When men do show up at a medical facility, according to Rhoades, they don't tend to mention specific ailments to the doctor unless the doctor specifically asks, which means that men must visit clairvoyants at the local Psychic Expo before receiving effective treatment.)

My father and my husband get along very well because at the end of the day, they're just two fallen-off heads sitting on the floor together in front of the TV, watching golf. My mother and I relate in a different way, which is that we pester each other incessantly with developments in health news, contacting each other by cellphone with snappy, tersely worded updates like a pair of FBI agents working a case. My mother sends me the Brown University health research newsletter every month, and also magazine and newspaper articles on new drugs for yeast infections and anxiety disorders and hangnails, while I report to her on what I've heard about colon cancer and conduct disorder and moles.

I find most of my news on the Net. Most women, I think I can safely say, are totally done in by the Internet when it comes to exploring their concerns about health. Let us say that one evening, after spending an hour in the bath washing the hair of eleven Barbies with my shampoo, my daughter, Clara, complains of "a pinchy feeling" in her bum. My first impulse will be to say, "Oh, I'm sure it will go away shortly." Because such things do. But then I'll get to thinking about it, and be up in my home office checking my email, and just start Web surfing a little bit on the matter of pinchy bums, and quickly lose touch with the space-time continuum. A study reported in 2004 by C & R Research in Chicago found that American mothers are now spending more than twice as much time online as they are watching television, and we all secretly know why this is. Officially, mothers report their Internet use as a timesaving measure. They need to cut to the chase. They need to Google "*Shrek* playing when?" and "Internet banking" and "old boyfriend from college: where now?" in two seconds flat.

But go on, just set "Dr. Mom" loose on a computer database that can access every medical library on the planet and see if she doesn't get as obsessed as any adolescent playing multi-player Dungeons & Dragons for thirteen days straight. One innocent symptom, like itching, can lead into a haunting catacomb of demonic illnesses and all of their prognoses and treatments. By two A.M. you're phoning a doctor: "My daughter is itchy—could she have this disease I've just learned about called onchocerciasis?" All mothers become the woman played by Susan Sarandon in that movie *Lorenzo's Oil,* who single-handedly researched her son's ultra-rare condition until she found a possible treatment. But none of us other mothers actually have a plausible illness to tackle; what we have is "eye aches" and "pinchy bums," and we can't figure out how to end the heroic maternal struggle and triumph with a conclusion, rather than Web-surf into infinity. So eventually, bleary-eyed, and fully aware that our husbands are watching golf with our fathers with their fallen-off heads on the floor, we throw up our hands and return to the Googled query: "Ex-boyfriend, where now?"

The Fastest Food in the West

The other day at the supermarket I noticed that boxes of microwave popcorn had been gathered up and plunked down in a sale bin near the checkout lines, as if on clearance. This wasn't surprising, given the headlines then blaring about microwave popcorn flavour vapours, which made everyone who had been attracted to the choice of instant popcorn suddenly run away.

What in God's name are "flavour vapours," you might ask. And I answer: I don't quite know. I can only say that the headlines referred to two employees at a food plant in Jasper, Missouri, who successfully sued International Flavors and Fragrances Inc. in 2003 for exposing them to a chemical that caused lung disease, and this chemical was involved in the production of synthesized flavours. The case provoked concern by authorities, worried, for instance, that the "butter flavour" fumes released when one opened a bag of microwaved popcorn could be hazardous to consumers who inhaled them.

Do you follow? Chemical plus fume equals clearance bin.

I don't know what they'll decide in the end, but meanwhile I can't help feeling blessed. I have narrowly averted the potential fate of microwave popcorn consumers simply because I've always felt that microwave popcorn was the world's most preposterous invention.

Here is how you make popcorn: Heat up corn kernels in some oil until they explode. Salt to taste.

Try this in a pot. You'll be surprised to find that it works exactly the same way as in a bag. Only it costs less. A bag of corn kernels will set you back roughly a dollar, and yield . . . I don't know . . . maybe twenty pots' worth of popcorn. The microwave version offers three bags for three times as much money. Is that convenience or bamboozlement?

Ah, but you want "butter flavour"? Actually, it's not a problem to achieve butter flavour with popcorn. Try melting butter! Pour it on your popcorn!

Not being a food historian, I don't know when, exactly, we started falling for the overblown seductions of food efficiency. Was it in the era of TV dinners? Of instant mashed potatoes? All I can tell you is that at some point we fell so hard for the pitch that we lost our capacity to do common evaluative comparisons. Microwave popcorn. Hmmm. Three dollars and three minutes. Regular popcorn. Hmmm. One dollar and three minutes. Of course, I would be an idiot if I wasn't a fan of labour-saving devices. I support improvements on the butter churn. But there were inventions along the way, one suspects, between the butter churn and organic, butter-flavoured, spray-on,

Canola oil that could have ended the labour issue in a satisfactory way. Cut blocks of butter on sale at the market would suffice, I would think, without plunging everyone's lives into perfidy and ruin.

Similarly, I don't want to keep egg-laying hens in my yard—how awkward—but still I have to say: Innovators, calm down. It isn't that arduous to drop store-bought eggs in boiling water and then peel them. I'm not convinced by the new Burnbrae Farms offering of already boiled eggs, now available by the half-dozen in the dairy section of my local supermarket. The pitch is elusive. No pot of water necessary! No peeling! Simply "rinse eggs before using."

Thanks, but no.

Tempting as it may be, I would have to be unconscious or hog-tied to benefit from that level of convenience in my kitchen. On the other hand, in the name of journalism, I decided to see if I could, in fact, prepare an egg salad sandwich while lying face down on the floor. So I took those already boiled eggs home and mixed in mayo from my new squeeze bottle of Hellmann's—no need for a knife! Just flip the cap open with your teeth, squeeze onto rinsed eggs, plant your face in the bowl, and stir with your nose! Eat with your mouth!

Too lazy to cook with pots? Afraid of microwave flavour vapours? Try our new, precut roast chicken in a thermo-lined sack! Just tie to your head and slurp!

There is a conflagration in the marketing, you have probably noticed, between the idea of efficiency and the myth of being on the go. Marketers don't want to suggest that people are lazy, so instead they characterize us as cheerfully active. Too busy and hurried to eat the old-fashioned way. Need feed bags now. No time for utensils. Gimme one of those yogurts in a tube.

This is how we arrive at oatmeal that is no longer merely instant but also portable, in the form of "Oatmeal to Go" breakfast bars, currently being advertised on TV by depicting someone jogging while eating a bowl of hot oatmeal. Like they can't get up five minutes earlier to turn on the kettle? Or consider Kraft Foods' latest innovation, Easy Mac. Kraft long ago usurped the world's simplest dinner, of boiled macaroni with cheese sauce. But wait! It turns out that maybe Kraft Dinner was too time-consuming. So the kitchen geniuses at Kraft slaved away, sensitive to the harried lives of working mothers and tube-fed teenagers, and came up with Easy Mac. Save minutes! Just stick the ingredients together in the microwave!

Not that they are abandoning their original KD. Far from it, there is a new ad campaign for that, too, where teens toss KD into a blender and then slurp the liquefied results from a tube.

To Market, to Market, 'Cause I'm a Fat Pig

A few years ago, pundits like me were warning of the logical extremes to which health fanaticism would lead. "What's next?" we demanded. "Lawsuits against the purveyors of fattening foods?"

We were merely being rhetorical. We certainly didn't hope to be prescient. So it was with some alarm that I reported the launching of a class-action lawsuit in New York in 2002 by a gaggle of plump people with heart disease, against a group of fast-food franchises that stood accused of giving them heart disease by making them plump.

Burger King, Wendy's, KFC, and McDonald's were being sued for failing to inform people that their burgers, fries, and buckets of chicken were fattening. (Note that KFC no longer goes by the name Kentucky Fried Chicken. Now the *F* can stand for something else, by inference, such as Fowl.)

The most publicly ridiculed among the plaintiffs of this lawsuit was Caesar Barber of the Bronx, who sat for an interview with Fox News that I watched after an episode of *Fear Factor* in which four people chewed live crickets in order to win a new car. Barber explained that he had had a heart attack as a result of the sneaky salesmanship at Burger King, et al.

"There was no fast food I didn't eat," Barber said, "and I ate it more often than not because I was single, it was quick, and I'm not a very good cook." Barber had already, perhaps unconsciously, built an air of haplessness into his public persona. No admission there of actually just loving double cheeseburgers and crispy fries. He was lonely! In a hurry! Couldn't figure out his microwave! The manufacturers of Kraft Dinner and McCain's Superfries must have been wiping their brows with a towel. What if Barber had sorted out how to boil water or turn his oven to 400 degrees?

Offering a defence where none was really necessary, a Wendy's employee told the *Boston Globe* at the time that she kept a stack of nutrition guides on hand, and her customers were free to eat the stuffed baked potatoes and fresh salads instead of ordering a combo.

I never did see any comment from McDonald's. Doubtless the fellows at the head office were sitting around in a collective clinical depression after settling a multi-million-dollar lawsuit earlier that year for falsely claiming that their French fries were "vegetarian."

Not surprisingly—for those of us who think that the logical extremes in society play out like slow-motion train wrecks—new lawsuits were quickly afoot against the manufacturers of sugar-free aspartame, high-fat health-food cheesies, alcohol companies, alternative medicine proprietors, and pharmaceutical manufacturers.

My favourite suit was brought by Meredith Berkman of New York City in 2002 against Robert's American Gourmet Foods, for mislabelling the fat content in Pirate's Booty, a pious health food store staple for neurotic parents whose children want cheesies.

Pirate's Booty, which my son tends to eat as an entree, is a pretend-cheesie product made of puffed rice and real cheddar cheese, as opposed to cornmeal and plutonium. Berkman headed a class-action suit accusing the company of misleading the public by labelling Pirate's Booty as "low-fat." Plaintiffs sought $50 million for "emotional distress and nutritional damage," according to news reports.

Nutritional damage? If these people can be emotionally distressed and nutritionally damaged by a rice puff, imagine what would happen to them in a war. Try suing the government of Sudan for forcing you to eat nothing but boiled shoe leather until everyone in your extended family dies.

Quarrels rage unabated in nutritional circles about whether carbohydrates or fats are the culprits in obesity, while potato growers try desperately to cultivate low-carb potatoes even as the purveyors of ice cream continue to stock the shelves with fat-free vanilla. Not even the traditional health food pioneers, whom we fondly call "the granola type," are immune. Britain's Food Commission recently announced that most brands of granola are fattening. Ha, ha. Here we have the eponymous health nut pooh-poohing the likes of burger-chomping Caesar Barber, and it turns out there are more grams of fat and sugar in some leading granola cereals than one finds in a slice of chocolate cake.

At least anti-smoking research is coherent. The food fights are a mess.

"McDonald's Corp.," declared a 2003 press release, "has enlisted the aid of Oprah Winfrey's personal trainer Bob Greene to promote an adult version of the Happy Meal, the fast-food giant's latest effort to offer healthier products. Instead of Happy Meal standards like a burger and a toy, the new Go Active meal will include a salad, an exercise booklet and a pedometer meant to encourage walking."

That's inventive of them, don't you think? Mind you, the skeptical part of my brain does wish to point out that McDonald's has now officially lost its way in the world of marketing, if it fails to understand that an exercise booklet makes a meal about as happy as being offered roast chicken with a hair shirt. Needless to say, if you want to make adults happy, give them a baby-sitting coupon. Or a joint. On the other hand, the meal has been endorsed by *Oprah Winfrey's* personal trainer. That's a Go Active meal with a whiff of glamour. A hint to all future Caesar Barbers. Fat? You coulda had a pedometer.

Cigarettes and Chocolate Milk

When people quit smoking, I strongly recommend that they join a gym. That way they can feel good about quitting and also feel an extra thrill of righteousness about making a monthly donation to a fitness centre they never attend. It works really well. Certainly in my case, after I foreswore my beloved Marlboro Lights and then immediately, with bright and happy intent, bought a pass to the YWCA, I felt marvellous. I don't regret the fifteen pounds I've gained since then. Not for a minute. Because, think about it. I *quit smoking* after twenty-three years! If part of that difficult, painful process involves throwing good money after bad, month after month after month, not going to the gym while slowly inflating like a hot air balloon, then so be it. I deserve to cut myself some slack. Or at very least to buy roomier pants.

By the way, I have a theory about the dramatic and unprecedented rise in obesity in our society, which is that the trend corresponds with the decline in smoking. Everyone is stopping their filthy habit and getting fat, just like me! Consider the math. In 1975, just under half of us smoked and less than a quarter of us were obese. Thirty years later the numbers have neatly reversed themselves. The hysterias have supplanted one another. Oh no! We're fat! We're all going to die! We quit smoking, but it doesn't matter, because we're fat and we're all going to die!

For a while I did try to curb my thigh inflation by playing tennis. The idea of this game entered my life in the excited yet nerve-racking run-up to quitting smoking, when everyone advised me to develop a new lifestyle with different rituals. It was a period not dissimilar to pregnancy, when those around me crowed with pleasure and offered a nostalgic knowledge.

"Oh! You're going to have so much more energy, you won't believe it!"

"You will be able to smell again, it's the greatest thing."

"Kissing tastes nicer."

"You just feel so much better about yourself. So much better."

I was encouraged to imagine stuff to do every hour and every minute and every second of every day that was jarringly new and that I wouldn't associate with smoking. I compiled a list. Don't go to bars. Join the gym. Don't go out for dinner. Sign up for tennis. Shun coffee shops. Arrange for dance lessons. Avoid writer friends. Hang out with joggers. Keep emotional turmoil to a minimum. And for God's sake, Patricia, *don't sit at your laptop and write another book.*

Originally, of course, my plan was to knock myself unconscious with a mallet shortly after breakfast each day.

But Ambrose felt supportive of tennis, having himself played all through high school. One day, as we found ourselves in Toys "R" Us, beating our zombie-like children back from the shelves with sticks, Ambrose cried, "Hey, look, they've got tennis rackets!" and grabbed one, which he threw into the cart with the Play-Doh and dinosaurs and Scrabble for Juniors. "It's on sale," he added. "This is actually a great price for a racket."

You know, you worry that these things are going to be inordinately complicated, these changes in lifestyle, and it's so pleasing and surprising when they're not. Who would have imagined that it would be easy peasy to transform myself from Christopher Hitchens into Billie Jean King in a happy matter of days? Of course, it's not that simple for the naturally sports-hostile, but I had always been athletic. It was a talent I had surpressed by sighing, swirling ice cubes in my cocktail, and smoking for decades. But it was still in me, the God-given grace, coordination, and gumption. I just wouldn't have talked myself back into it but for Ambrose and his casual, comfortable sports *savoir faire*.

The next weekend I donned my tennis whites, stuffed a tube of balls into my purse, grabbed the sheathed racket, and headed off to the Cottingham Tennis Club on a leafy residential street in wealthy North Toronto. Look at me, off to play tennis! I parked my cherry-red Mazda and hopped out, experimenting with my level of energy. Could I reclaim the happy skip of my youth, or was that too wishful? I was worried, in truth, that I didn't have the right shoes on. When I entered the white wooden clubhouse lit with sunshine, I asked the resident tennis pro at the club, a young man who was as handsome and cheery as Reggie in the Archie comics.

"You're fine," he said. Then he paused mid-stride out the clubhouse door and looked at me more hesitantly. "I guess you realize that you've got a children's racket?" I stared at the object hanging from my shoulder, shocked. "Do I? My husband bought it for me." My husband's *a guy*. They know their sports.

"Where did he buy it?" the pro asked, curious.

"Oh," the answer thwacked me in the face. "Well. Toys 'R' Us." Even as the reply came out of my mouth, my face began burning and my game partner, S., brayed with laughter.

What could I do? We were there. We were dressed. So, I played. I went out there onto that clay court shaded by maple trees, between a hard-fought doubles game involving a quartet of age-defiant seniors, and a singles match between two strapping college men straight out of *Chariots of Fire*. I strode out with dignified determination, refusing to concern myself with the pointed stares of tennis snobs, and whacked at the balls with my dorky plastic racket until I ruined my wrist, which took about fifteen minutes. After that, I found it difficult to exaltedly fling myself into the sport of tennis because I kept not having time to get to a proper store and buy a proper racket.

Nevertheless, I did alter my routine. There was still that pressing necessity of the ex-smoker, to climb the walls of one's house, bug-eyed, and head out the window and onto the roof, there to either jump off or find a new mode of being in the world.

Now when I rise in the morning and pour my coffee, instead of reaching for a cigarette, I whip out a pen and write a to-do list that invariably starts with the phrase: "Go to the gym" and then continues, in parentheses, underlined twice, "or at least resume tennis." You *loser*.

Then I eat a lot.

So what has kept me on the wagon, you might well ask. It is no easy task, I am telling you, and that is not because I am an immoral half-demon in lust with debauchery. It is because nicotine is very (squared) addictive. Only three percent of smokers quit successfully on a given try. *Three percent.* That is why it's taken half a century to reduce the smoking rates. But there's a reason for this. It's because nicotine is very, very, very, very addictive, I don't know if I mentioned that. The brain thinks that nicotine is super. Jettison tobacco from your mind and just think nicotine. Nicotine, nicotine, nicotine, nicotine. What a nice, subtle drug. It doesn't make you paranoid, like pot, or violent, like alcohol, or aimlessly emotive like ecstasy. It sharpens your memory and clarifies your thoughts. It soothes your anxiety and lifts your depression. In pure form, nicotine is efficacious, and just about as harmless and as addictive as caffeine.

What to do? Unhitch it from its lethal harness, and in a rational society, such as Sweden, that would just be a matter of: Off you go and have fun with your Nicorette gum or what have you. The Swedes have figured this all out and cut their smoking rates in half by introducing—among many other things—Snus, a form of miniature nicotine tea bag that former Swedish smokers place between their gums and their lips.

Since I quit, my cousin has fallen off the wagon and done a face plant and so have two of my friends. I figure this is because none of them opted, as I did, for Nicotine Replacement Therapy. For Snus and its variants. Also known as NRT. Smoker's methadone. The patch, the gum, the spray, the inhaler, the lozenge, the mallet. To quit smoking on the first try, you must surround yourself with these NRTs until you're swimming in the stuff, never more than six inches away from a dose of nicotine. If you don't believe me, ponder the three percent statistic I just cited.

This is the secret of my success, and I wish to emphasize the word *secret* because very few people have figured out the usefulness of NRTs, particularly here in Canada where very few are available. Health bureaucrats haven't noticed, yet, that if you immerse ex-smokers in a vat of liquid nicotine forever, they will remain content. Dose them, and they will fail to succumb to cancer, heart disease, respiratory crisis, impotence, jaundice, narcolepsy, frostbite, cramps, and soul-crushing guilt. It's true! You will get rid of those perils by altering their "nicotine delivery system," and all that ex-smokers will be left with is the ignominy of getting fat and the quandary of not knowing where to put their chewed gum.

How to Get Hives Trying to Follow News of Cancer

The *New England Journal of Medicine* recently reported that "longer-legged people are significantly more prone to certain types of cancer." Indeed. Well, that's just a huge relief for me. I can never see over anybody's head in a crowd. I suppose I'll just fry up another carcinogenic burger on my barbecue and snicker at the supermodels. Or not. How do I make use of this news, really? Here I was, feeling dismay at an entirely different bit of tall-people research, in which I'd just heard on the radio that the long-legged win promotions more often at work. And now it emerges that their good fortune is undermined by their greater risk of perishing from lymphoma. Which suggests that appraising your fate strictly from the vantage point of your legs is a zero-sum game.

So, for that matter, is appraising your chances of cancer, for science pelts us daily with new studies on everything that prevents it, and everything that promotes it, and everything that they thought caused cancer before but now realize actually prevents it, and vice versa. At the moment, for example, I have been given to understand that if I stay short, drink red wine, eat tomatoes, use olive oil, cease working in a coke foundry, avoid cigars, sleep more, take Aspirin—or, no, that's been shown to cause pancreatic cancer—take less Aspirin, swallow Vitamin E, alter my estrogen levels, sip green tea, shun charcoal briquettes, dine on fish—but not from the Great Lakes—reduce my stress level, find religion, and stay clear of Eastern Europe, my chances of dying from cancer will be reduced. For the time being.

But it turns out that the sunblock that I've been smearing all over my arms for five years may be carcinogenic, whereas sunshine is now thought to act as a cancer preventive. Meanwhile, the spinach and apples I've been eating all these years to bust cancer are laden with cancer-causing pesticide residues. Likewise, Vitamin C, long touted as an antioxidant par excellence in megadoses, may actually change the structure of our DNA in such a way that—no, you didn't guess, did you?—it makes us more susceptible to cancer. And those soft plastic dishes I've been using to microwave my anticancer vegetables in? They cause cancer.

Every now and then, a cancer-fighting diet book comes out, and I've noticed that the author has an extremely narrow window of opportunity, maybe three days, to sell out the print run before a squadron of doctors charges forth to the media mikes to repudiate all of its findings. Isn't that great? I wanted to phone my mother to tell her how I've had it up to here (writer's hand slicing sideways at chin level) with trying to keep track of every eensy-weensy obscure bit of research on health perils. But I'd just read that cellphones were being implicated in brain tumours. I sent her a note.

"It seems to me," I wrote her, "that what this whole explosion in medical research is actually discovering is that sooner or later people die."

Of course, scientists are finding out other things that are useful to them, but they are not very useful to me. What all this research is generating in people is the expectation that somehow they don't have to die—that if only they can get *all the information*, they can beat the odds. If you talk to an insurance actuary, you'll be told what people actually die of, cancer-wise: everything and nothing. Plus smoking. Smoking is way, way up there with car accidents and heart attacks as a cause of death. And you know what to do about that one. Every other prevention strategy, in my opinion, is a crapshoot.

From now on, I follow the only recipe for longevity that's ever actually made sense to me: moderation in all things. A little wine, a nice walk, a good dish of pasta, a minimal amount of microwaving in Tupperware containers, a dash of olive oil, a soupçon of Vitamin C, a very brief visit to Eastern Europe. Live life modestly, except during the holidays and when you're depressed or bored or having marital troubles, and then hope for the best. It is, after all, not a life worth living if it is lived only to see just how long it can last.

CHOICES WE DON'T CARE TO MAKE

Top Ten Toys in the Pearson Household

'Tis the Season for Hottest Toy Lists, la la la la la, la la la laaaa.

Oh Lord, I hate these Christmas lists. They correspond not at all to what my children play with the whole year through. The toys the stores promote are trumped-up, fleeting, and a colossal waste of cash because most of them are electronic and last approximately forty-eight hours before getting trashed or disembowelled.

Consider this one toy I came across called Commando-bot, a plaything that contains more sophisticated gadgetry than my 2003 Mazda. Commandobot responds to voices. If I was coming down the hall, for example, Commandobot might burble "Help! Help! Don't throw me in the trash!" To which I—responding to its deeply annoying vocal timbre with my own built-in capacity to distinguish sounds—would say: "The trash is too good for you, toy, you're going into the FIRE! Ha ha ha."

Honestly, I defy my fellow parents to think of a single electronic toy that hasn't driven them completely insane within hours, and whose batteries haven't either been ripped out and hidden or lost under the couch. What parent fails to anticipate the fate of Hokey Pokey Elmo in a house full of preschoolers, even as he or she forks over the dough for this waltzing puppet, currently claiming pride of place in *Toy Wishes* magazine's "hottest dozen"?

I know, *Sesame Street*'s Elmo seems cute, and the song is endearing . . . at first. But, let me tell you, I've had a bouncing Tigger in my home for several years now that has become as familiar a bit of detritus as dust balls and never-used extension cords. I come across it weekly actually, on Saturdays, in my attempt to move Useless Things to new Useless Thing Containers. When I try to throw it out, my daughter intervenes on the magpie principle. It glimmered once, this Tigger, for roughly two weeks, and so she cannot let it go. I replaced the batteries once, thinking that would thrill her. She made Tigger bounce for five minutes and then ignored him again. But I am a chump, and honour her nostalgia.

For the record, here are the ten hottest toys in the Pearson household:

- A stick found in the park. This comes in a variety of wood hues and is, ideally, three or four feet long with shorter versions available after the prolonged temper tantrum about huge stick's inability to fit into the car. Sticks can function as a dragon to menace one's elder sister, can be poked into desiccated mice, and can be rattled along a picket fence.
- The phone. This is a versatile object that rings and has

buttons. The receiver can be picked up and put down again to miraculously end the ringing noise. The buttons can be punched endlessly, dialling 911, and 411, and the mayor. The cord can be attached to the dog as a leash. Six-hour conversations with fellow adolescents can take place from the comfort of one's own bed. Recommended for children aged one to eighteen.

- A bottle of Lancôme nail polish. Possibilities include hiding the nail polish in a boot and applying its contents to doll's lips, the cat's tail, or one's pants.
- Toilet paper. Several uses. Damp spitballs, fake breasts, Barbie bedding, bathtub experiments, cardboard role turned into telescope. Simple act of unfurling and trailing all the way down the stairs will entertain kids for as long as it takes a parent to notice.
- A sack of Robin Hood flour, a spoon, the garden hose, and a pot. Add twigs, paint, chewed gum, or other easily available ingredients to taste.
- The cat. Preferably asleep and therefore willing to wear a kerchief and be transported in a stroller.
- Dirt. A chestnut found on the sidewalk. Fantasies of planting said chestnut in the dirt and waking up to a fifty-foot tree.
- Food. No toy beats mashed-potato sculpting with "found objects," such as one's thumb or a pen on the kitchen table. Mashed-potato accessories, like ketchup, sold separately.
- The Internet. Outlasts the Energizer Bunny.
- Dollar-store stuff. Perfect. Quality matches attention span.

Under the circumstances, I now resent practically every toy I have bought for my children and proceeded to trip over, retrieve from the toilet, or find caked in dirt in the garden. The entire Christmas shopping exercise seems to me to have become a process of alienating parents from their own progeny, in order to fulfill commercially pushed fashions.

Needless to say, this is not done for the benefit of parents or children but for the ongoing health of the toy industry. Consider the practice of brand extension, which is a marketing concept in which you take one reliable product and spin it off in endless variations. Apply this concept to the old kitchen play-set. A standard play-set, involving sink, oven, and fridge all rolled into one object, can last for years, which isn't good for the toy industry. So now, if you peruse the toy store shelves or watch TV commercials, you'll note the plastic fridge, the pretend microwave oven, and—for parents who have totally lost their minds—the pie cabinet at Pottery Barn Kids, which will wind up concealing the toothpaste and cooked squash sauce that your child whipped up experimentally and then hid—until you began rooting around her room trying to locate *that godawful smell.*

Whatever happened to the world so magically invoked in the book series *Little House on the Prairie,* in which the excitement of Christmas involved receiving fresh oranges and handmade doll quilts? Gone: a vanished era of keeping material wealth in perspective.

The great irony of this is that children themselves are

capable of keeping wealth in perspective, in the sense that they can rest content with far less than what we shower upon them. True, they will jump up and down in glee when you present them with the Barbie "Cook with Me" Smart Kitchen that they saw advertised on TV. But they're just game for the hype. Otherwise, they achieve marvels with sticks. It is our job, not theirs, to stand back and ask ourselves what we wish for ourselves as families in a resource-scarce world.

Shop and Do Twenty

Christmas is almost upon us. I know this because TV commercials tell me so, as do the garish displays of gift baskets in my supermarket. Christmas is coming, they all shout in chorus. Time to buy things!

On Christmas Eve, as is my tradition, I will be found standing around dumbfounded in a mall, having been unable until then to decide upon gifts for at least three people. Then, staggering home with the last of my frantic acquisitions, I will plan to go to midnight Mass and cross my fingers that I'm not too exhausted to pay my respects to God.

The collision between commercialism and spirituality is never so extreme as during this particular season, when we profit and worship with equal fervour. It is a pairing of objectives so opposite to each other that it builds a unique sort of stomach-clenching stress. America is simultaneously the most religious of the great Western nations and also the most consumer-driven.

Hence, the stress of holiday shopping, as Webb Keane, an anthropologist at the University of Michigan, pointed out to me recently, involves the desire we feel to honour the spirit of Christmas by giving gifts—which is to say tokens of love that are meaningful, thoughtful, personal— and the fact that we have to choose those gifts from a vast, impersonal array of mass-produced goods.

"The anxiety is not really about the crowds and getting to the store," Keane says, "but trying to resolve the contradiction between the social meaning of Christmas and the anonymous, even alienating nature of commodities."

If we didn't feel so ambivalent about the purpose of holiday shopping, Keane told me, we would simply exchange money orders. Alternatively, we would skip gift giving altogether and enjoy our friends and relatives, as we do at Thanksgiving.

Instead, we go to great, headache-inspiring lengths to find the perfect doll or sweater, and then conceal the material nature of the objects we've bought by, for instance, removing the price tag and wrapping them. *Look, honey! I've bought you a mass-produced sweater from Banana Republic, but I slid it inside coloured paper myself!*

Shopping anxiety increases exponentially, or so it seems to me, when we don't have the time or the energy to truly personalize our gift giving—a quandary that is increasingly true for women, the traditional gift givers, who are caught more and more in the work-family timebind.

I was reminded of this when I stood mindlessly gazing around in a book superstore one weekend, paralyzed at the prospect of browsing through hundreds of thousands of titles. I noticed a book called *Simplify Your Christmas* and wanted to pick it up, but I was carrying a to-do list, a gift basket, a bag of takeout food, a door wreath, and my briefcase, and didn't have any hands. Also, I had no time.

Just then, I spied a time-management guide, which distracted me for about ten seconds—long enough to forget where I'd seen *Simplify Your Christmas*.

I tried to find it again, but after scanning twelve shelves with my head bent sideways, I developed neck pain and had to sit down. Luckily, I was in the self-help section.

How to Thrive When the World Overwhelms You, one title beckoned, as if it wasn't partly the fault of that very book, barking for my attention in this enormous chorus of woof-woofery.

What about a book called *How to Do Christmas Shopping Without Being Confronted by 411,000 Product Options per Square Block*? Where's that title?

The tension of Christmas shopping may be a "perennial complaint," as Keane argues, but never before have retailers clamoured so relentlessly, pushing—through gigantic malls and superstores—a volume of product so overwhelming that it oppresses the soul.

In what has now become the most prolonged product boom in American history, we are strapped for time and overloaded with choices. The average supermarket currently offers sixty thousand products. (I am bewildered at a dairy counter, merely pondering brands of cheese.)

Companies that used to offer one type of soup or toothpaste now have up to a dozen variations: Colgate Baking Soda & Peroxide Whitening with tartar control, Crest extra whitening with tartar protection, Ultra Brite advanced whitening, Colgate Total, and . . . *bleh* . . . I'll just brush my teeth with twigs.

Add to this, if you dare, entire categories of retail merchandise that didn't exist when our parents were shopping: product tie-ins with film and TV shows, for instance. There's an entire contingent of furtive mothers out there—I've met two of them recently—who are snaking past the McDonald's drive-thru window twice on a given day in order to get the second and third toy in the Happy Meal product tie-in lineup.

The whole enterprise of shopping, which we are being encouraged more and more emphatically to engage in to bolster the economy, has grown strangely disempowering, as if the freedom to choose has been overridden by the compulsion to choose whatever is pushed in our faces.

E-commerce has added its own potent fuel to this fire of abundance. At one time if you wished to buy a book for your beloved, there was pleasure and solace to be found around the corner at the local bookshop, where a clerk could chat knowledgeably with you about literature. On the Net, books are available by the oceanic ton. One company, Advanced Book Exchange (www.abebooks.com) offers nearly eleven million titles from its global network of dealers. The Net effect? How can you fail to come up with the "perfect" present when you have access to everything ever printed or made?

Add to this, finally, another stress factor: As Keane noted, "our sense of community is even more unstable and fractured than it was before." If Christmas is about our efforts to forge relationships with one another, then shopping, when our relationships are that much more tenuous, far-flung, and delicately in need of tending, is all the more fraught with anxiety.

The solution, for me at least, will be to make donations to charity on behalf of those I love and otherwise raise a toast of good cheer to them all.

Beauty Shop Bullies

I have stumbled across a book, *Why We Buy: The Science of Shopping,* that finally explains why I would rather be stuck in an elevator with bees than shop for cosmetics.

According to the author, Paco Underhill, fancy-ass makeup sold at gleaming department store counters by what he calls "the dolls in the official white lab coats (and Saturday-night-out makeup)" make women like me feel like dirt. On purpose. It's a sales strategy.

Why am I not surprised?

"This is the high-pressure school of cosmetics selling," Underhill, a retail anthropologist, reveals. "You sit on the stool, she turns you into a slightly toned-down version of herself, and you buy what she urges on you (in theory, at least). The prices are intentionally obscure, figuring that you'll be too intimidated to ask."

Isn't that exactly right? What woman but Nicole Kidman has ever felt comfortable entering the perfumed zone of department stores, with their cold chrome counters and ultra-polished saleswomen, who remind you of the cool girls in high school who knew how to put on eyeliner without looking like hungover raccoons?

I always feel like a loser at makeup counters. One minute I'm strolling through the hosiery section in an upbeat mood, and the next thing I know I'm at the Lancôme counter staring into the huge blown-up face of Elizabeth Jagger. I instantly feel so unfashionable that it seems impudent for me even to be there, let alone solicit the attention of the Cool Girls.

It's like a hostile little ecosystem of female rivalry, with a smell of sugar-coated bitchiness in the air, which is what I always think of when I sniff Poison and Eternity.

So, over the years, I've reduced my cosmetics purchases to two items: Lancôme's Intencils mascara, which I can dart in, grab, and dart out again with, never having asked the price, and M·A·C's Twig lipstick, ditto.

Another problem women face in the cosmetics bazaar, Underhill points out, is that "manufacturers and retailers want to sell the products in as clean and orderly a way as possible." Women, however, "want to try before they buy, which is not always a clean and orderly impulse. The interest of seller and buyer shouldn't be at odds, but often, they are."

Indeed, who wants to hang around being stared at by a Cool Girl while trying to imagine what "hydrating and matifying long-lasting treatment oil-free fresh gel" feels like without being able to touch it?

Not only does the anal-retentive environment remind you of standing in your boyfriend's mother's kitchen during college, noticing that the bananas are Saran-wrapped and wondering if you dare have a snack, but the products are mystifying.

How, without sampling, are you supposed to decide between Lancôme's four types of "cleanser with water," two "without water," four toners, two makeup removers, four exfoliators, and three hand creams? Certainly not from their names, which are a ludicrous jumble of pseudo-science and quasi-French. What is Hydra Controle? Is it the same thing as Primordiale Nuit? Do I wish to ask the Cool Girl? No, I do not.

Later, I learned from Lancôme's website that Primordiale Nuit results in "soft and appeased skin" due to the cream's unique delivery system of "nanocapsules" of Vitamin A. I did not learn the price.

Underhill has done a study of women's behaviour in drugstore cosmetics aisles and determined that female shoppers like to study the information on product packaging before they buy. (And you wonder why.) Perhaps for this reason, more and more cosmetics companies are going online, where women can ponder the offerings at their leisure.

Also, according to Underhill, some makeup retailers have been persuaded by market research to switch to an "open sell" strategy, in which the lipsticks and shadows are available for handling and sampling, rather than being locked in cases as if women were dirty toddlers not to be trusted.

Cosmetics bazaars are still nowhere near the level of comfort you feel in some record stores now, where you can listen to CDs entirely unobserved, potentially for hours. But if they were, you wouldn't be too intimidated to ask the price, now, would you? Ah, the beauty myth— exploiting it can be such a tricky job.

Shave and a Haircut

I had my hair cut in a barber shop the other day. I know that's a bit of a transgression for a female. But I needed to do it. I finally just refused to fork over seventy-five dollars plus tip merely to lose two inches straight off the back.

I have been envying my husband for years on this count—the way he just strolls home with a spontaneously acquired haircut, as casually purchased as batteries from the corner store. He gets his hair cut without thinking about it twice, as if out to mow the lawn or sheer a sheep. "Less hair, please. Thank you, here is eleven dollars."

By contrast, I find haircuts to be a deeply tormenting experience. I never find the right stylist. Every six months I begin all over again by carefully scrutinizing the hair of every woman I know, then interrogating them about their stylist until I'm satisfied that the stylist in question will actually do something competent to my head in exchange for a great deal of money.

I arrive at the hair salon, which reeks of aromatherapy, and check in with a receptionist who sports a nose jewel and has some wholly indefinable way of making me feel as if I do not belong to her club because, well, *just look at my dorky hair*. Then I have to change out of my clothes and don a cranberry-coloured robe, as if I'm about to undergo a CAT scan. Thus stripped of whatever personality I can project through personal fashion, I discuss numerous haircuts with a sycophantic stylist, who is really just pondering my face in his hotly unflattering lights and thinking that it's irredeemably loaf-shaped.

Having arrived at some inscrutable decision about how, precisely, he is going to cut two inches off the back of my hair, he turns me over to an eighteen-year-old in three-storey-high platform shoes, who starts massaging my hands with aromatherapeutic almond-scented oil, making them so slippery that I can't grip my coffee mug.

I get escorted to the sinks to have my hair lathered with Product, even if I have washed it already that day, and for the ensuing hour, the highly fashionable stylist clips microscopic strands of hair from all over my head while engaging in forced banter.

"Who trimmed your bangs—they look fabulous."

"I did, with nail scissors."

Silence.

"So, what do you do?"

"I'm a writer."

"Oh cool."

Silence.

"Do you ever dream," I ask sometimes, trying to hot-wire the conversation, "that you're cutting someone's hair, only instead of using scissors, you find that you're holding a stalk of asparagus or something?"

"No, not really."

Silence.

I can't read because the stylist wants my head up straight, so I have to stare into the mirror at all times. It's like the stylist is shouting "Look at yourself! Look. At. Yourself." It reminds me of that classic *Saturday Night Live* skit, in which a drill sergeant is haranguing his recruits by calling them names; he says to one of them: "You! Yeah, you. You with that . . . hair . . . on your head. Know what I'm gonna call you? HAIR HEAD."

I walk out with a "hairdo" that falls apart as soon as I wash out the conditioner/touch of mousse/finishing spray that has propped it up like egg white in meringue.

Some women love going to the hair salon, I realize, so I should point out that I have straight super-fine hair. There is simply nothing you can do with straight super-fine hair that makes any difference if you don't have a one-inch wide face. If your cheekbones aren't apparent, and your chin doesn't end in a piquant point like Gwyneth Paltrow's, then this kind of hair is going to be the bane of your existence no matter how much cash you have. I always leave feeling disappointed and shafted, and over the years, the intervals between salon visits has been lengthening.

Finally, the moment of eureka. I went to a barber. Mind you, this was easier to conceive of than to execute. It took me weeks to pluck up my courage. But at last I felt bold (or desperate) enough to walk into Enzo's Hairstyles for

Men, a plain room in Toronto's Little Italy, which was truthfully and indeed very clearly marked Enzo's Hairstyles for Men. I sat down in an old vinyl chair beside a stack of *Sports Illustrated* magazines and waited my turn. Enzo, barber and proprietor, nodded at me courteously when he spied me on the chair. He didn't seem to balk at my presence. It was all about my own confidence, I felt certain. All I had to do was get over the feeling that I had walked into Enzo's Hairstyles for Men, and I would be free. Free at last!

Enzo was attired in pale yellow work shirt and grey pants. He could as easily have been a hardware store manager. He was using a straight razor on a sallow young man with round wire-rimmed spectacles who was dressed all in black and seemed penniless, perhaps scribbling away at a novel. Another fellow waiting for a cut was burly and macho in his soiled white T-shirt—perhaps a mechanic. It occurred to me that the last thing these three men had in common was an interest in fashion. On the other hand, they were having a great, animated conversation about who was destined to win the World Cup.

"Spain," vowed Enzo.

"Argentina for sure," offered the burly man.

"I think Somalia might stay in the game," said the probable-novelist, just to be provocative.

They all pooh-poohed the Portuguese, who were just then cruising by with horns a-blazing, having beaten the Poles in a match.

"So what?" said the burly fellow.

"They're going to start a fight with the Italians around here." Enzo seemed worried.

The walls, I noticed, were festooned with posters of Italian soccer players and Canadian hockey stars. None of them had visibly styled hair. A tinny radio played golden oldies somewhere in the back, primarily for the entertainment of Enzo. He was smoking. That was how the room smelled—faintly of smoke, then more strongly of coffee, and the breeze of a fine June morning.

When my turn came, I hopped into his worn-leather barber chair, and Enzo covered me with a linen cloth.

"Two inches off the back," I announced.

He swivelled the chair away from the mirror, calmly and gently combed my dry hair, and snipped. *Snip, snip, snip.* It took five minutes. Cost fifteen dollars. Praise the Lord, I'm free at last.

Buy Toothpaste, Call Dad, Plan Funeral for Self

Lately, I've been getting these flyers in the mail from local funeral homes that cheerfully encourage me to come in and arrange my own burial. I find this a bit disconcerting. I have many things on my to-do list: Enroll daughter in summer camp, buy husband birthday present, stop skipping yoga class, read Tolstoy, figure out why God made dinosaurs. "Plan funeral for self" isn't one of them.

Obviously the funeral industry thinks that it should be, because I get these flyers, and I noticed a big ad in the paper recently that promised anyone who bought a cemetery plot the chance to win a Carribean cruise. Pay now, die later! But, for God's sake, pay now.

Trying to figure out how this would benefit me, as opposed to the funeral industry, I went on the Internet and found a helpful website prepared by the Preplanning Network, an association of North American funeral homes engaged in the business of getting you to come in bursting with health and vitality to finalize the details of your death.

The site has a Procrastination Help Centre, which never actually mentions the words *death* or *funeral*. Instead, it gently points out that "people who procrastinate to excess are prone to nagging guilt, self-downing, anxiety and a numbing feeling of powerlessness."

Empower yourself: Rot your own way!

Not convinced?

Well, consider that the desperate fear of confronting one's own mortality—"I'm too young!"—is just one of "the most common excuses not to preplan," according to the Preplanning Network, whose members appear to have lost perspective about what motivates most of humanity. "The younger generations are the ones who will benefit the most from preneed funeral arrangements," the site argues. "With increasing funeral costs your services will be locked in."

Maybe they will. But surely the funeral people can come up with a more compelling incentive.

I decided to visit my local funeral home to find out what on earth they were trying to accomplish. Two "advance planning administrators" greeted me graciously in the silent beige-toned front parlour of Earle Elliott Funeral Home on Dovercourt Road in Toronto. They wore shades of grey and black, as did I, so we were all very appropriate. Funeral homes are nothing if not appropriate, which is why they have a hard time engaging in self-promotion: It's hardly appropriate at times like these.

"Funeral homes didn't traditionally advertise," Crystal Middelkamp told me, speaking in hushed tones, out of professional habit, "but they have become very concerned about educating the public."

"Educating them about what?" I asked in a normal voice, which somehow sounded like shouting.

"The value of having a service," she replied. For a while there, people were opting for simplicity, and that didn't work out. Not for them, and not—I presume—for the funeral industry, which is engaged in a frantic scrabble for business at the moment, with huge corporate chains like Service Corporation International (SCI) and The Loewen Group aggressively focusing on profit while small homes like this one fight back with their own competitive push. Or have you not been watching *Six Feet Under?*

According to the Funeral Consumers Alliance (FCA) in Hinesburg, Vermont, the Houston-based SCI distributed a company memo recently advising staff to bag one "preneeds contract" for every actual dead person. At several funeral homes, staffers now work on commission. Part of the issue is an industry out of kilter with demand: In New York State, 661 funeral homes are necessary to handle the population of deceased people every year, according to the FCA. But the state has 1,981 homes in operation. The ratio is similar in most other states, and probably also in Canada. How do you drum up nonexistent business? You get people to pay up before they're even dead.

"We offer a wide variety of services," Middelkamp went on. "Burial, cremation, church service, location of the ceremony—if you want to have a service on top of the CN Tower, we can do that. We've had people bring in items to display from home, favourite chairs, pictures, live jazz bands, pets . . ."

"The younger generation is starting to get imaginative," interjected Karie, Crystal's colleague. "The baby boomers expect a lot of choices because of their attitude as consumers."

This put me in mind of a custom-ordered casket company called White Light Inc. that operates out of Dallas. From them, you can order a coffin painted as a brown paper parcel with RETURN TO SENDER stamped on it in red letters. Har, har. Or if you were into the Indy 500, you could get a coffin with race cars zooming all over it. Hunters can choose a deer and rabbit motif; gardeners pick flowers. People used to be memorialized according to their virtues: the brave warrior, the wise ruler, the great poet. Now they head into eternity with Knit-Wit.

"But even if people want more ritual," I said, "why can't they jot it down in a will, or leave it to the family? Why do it themselves?" The short answer, according to Crystal, is that it's easier to shop when you're not grieving. "A lot of times, families come in [after the death] and they're totally overwhelmed. With preplanning, there's no rush, you can spend all afternoon, you're having a cup of tea and laughing. It's more relaxed."

Padding silently across the plush carpet, Crystal and Karie led me to inspect my options as a future dead person. I could, for example, choose from a few vaults, which are an increasingly popular accessory, although the only thing they accomplish is to ease cemetery maintenance by warding off grave cave-ins. If people are worried about their caskets decaying, in my opinion, they might consider burial in the tundra. I myself would like to be buried in a bed of soft lake sediment so that I can turn up in 215 million years as an interesting fossil. But that isn't the point of vaults, from a funeral home's point of view.

Near the vault models was a crucifix display, as well as some stationery, and a variety of guest books to choose from. *Hmmm.* The few times in my life that I've imagined my funeral, it has been a revenge fantasy, wherein an ex-boyfriend or nasty colleague stumbles into the church with teary eyes, regretting everything they said. I hadn't thought about stationery, or a guest book. I sometimes imagine what music I'd like people to be listening to as they mourn me, but I change my mind too often to "lock it in." (N.B. to self: Make sure family knows that I am not, under any circumstances, to be memorialized to the careering drone of Anglican hymns.)

We floated downstairs to the coffin display room. They all looked the same to me—bloody terrifying. What was the selection criteria? Was I supposed to lie down in each one to see which best flattered my corpse? I contemplated the Sheraton, a plum-coloured casket with pink satin lining. Then I mused over the Ladies Octagon Oak, with its embroidered roses. "You know what? Why don't you just bury me in a paper bag," I suggested.

Karie and Crystal immediately protested in hushed alarm. "But it's not for you—it's for your family! For the service, where they need support! They're going through the roughest days they'll ever face."

Oh geez, we come full circle then, don't we? If it's not for me, then someone else can plan it. And in the meantime, I can drive and cook dinner and dance as I fantasize about my all-time favourite send-off songs.

To Be Mrs. or Not to Be Mrs.

It seems to be growing fashionable again among educated women of my acquaintance to take their husband's surname after marching down the aisle. The Washington conservative writer Danielle Crittenden, who is married to George Bush's former speech writer David Frum, has observed that wives who insist on keeping their own names are simply engaging in a "display of insecurity."

That's an interesting thought. Call my preference for staying Pearson a sign of insecurity if you like, but my husband's last name is Pottie, and going through my life as Patty Pottie has about as much appeal to me as wearing a dunce cap to a ball.

Besides, I already have a name, as I see it, and my merger with my husband is symbolized in other ways, such as that I—and no other woman—get to wear his boxer shorts when all of my underwear is in the laundry. Also, of course, we have wedding rings, and a joint chequing account, and children with our blended DNA and their very own talent for tantrums, which my husband and I suffer through in tandem. So I tend to think of myself as fully and demonstrably merged.

Like everything else, the question of what a woman ought to do with her name upon donning her wedding gown has more than one answer in our culture. Some answers are highly inventive—such as a couple whose surnames were both colours, which they changed to the hue that those two colours created when mixed, which was, we hope, not puce. Other answers involve hyphens or an ungainly split between husband and pen name, or indeed the use of an alias.

If you're getting married and can't decide whether to be Mrs. His Wife, as the Washington pundit referred to herself, or instead Mrs. Beige, or The Jackal, perhaps you might consider the customs of other countries.

The Burmese, for example, have no last names, which makes these sorts of feminist quandaries irrelevant. Madonna could marry Fabio and not a single Burmese eyebrow would rise.

The Indian state of Kerala is a matrilineal culture, with property being passed down from mother to daughter. Thus, the men who marry in Kerala adopt their wives' names. They may or may not resent it—I couldn't find any reference to the debate in a scan of the *Times of India*.

Elsewhere in India, women keep their fathers' last names when they get married, whereas their husbands have reversed names. My husband and I, if married in Rajasthan, would become Patricia Pearson and Pottie Ambrose, which I would call a much better deal for me.

In other parts of India, on the other hand, it's more common for women to take their husband's names, although not always.

In Ethiopia a woman takes her father's first name as a lifelong moniker. If I were Ethiopian, my name would be Patricia Geoffrey, and my daughter would be Clara Ambrose instead of Clara Pottie, and marriage wouldn't alter that one way or the other.

Every Ethiopian name has a concrete meaning, like *potato* or *lion,* so tracing one's lineage backward means stringing words together to form an actual sentence. Instead of having a family coat of arms or other visual symbol for lineage, you get a phrase like "God's potato, eater of lions." The system is probably getting a bit mucked up by new generations of Ethiopians, mind you, who emigrate to Israel or England and marry men with names like Arnie.

But the basic objective is to convey blood lineage in one's name rather than husband-love, which is also true for women in Singapore and Taiwan, who keep their paternal surnames.

The Mexicans have managed to evolve a highly compli-cated naming custom, wherein a woman grows up with her father's last name followed by her mother's last name, which in my case would be Pearson Mackenzie. When she marries, she loses her father, adds her spouse, and moves her mother to the middle: Mackenzie Pottie. Partly for that reason, Mexican women generally prefer to go by their first names only, as in Doña Flora or Doña Sofia. Maybe that's what I should have done. I was born in Mexico, so I could appropriate the convention and walk around demanding to be called Doña Pat. Why not?

Or I could hyphenate the combination and show respect for both my lineage and my husband. From now on, I'm going to sign all documents "Mrs. His Wife-Doña Pat." What do you think?

The Illusion of Choice

Lately I've been wondering, whatever happened to that press conference that Bill Gates gave a few years ago, in which he announced his intention to develop software that could connect my oven to the Internet? No further explanation was proffered in any of the news accounts that I read at the time. Nevertheless, for some reason, in the exciting near future, if Gates carries through on his vision, my oven will download recipes directly from the World Wide Web to itself.

Well, if Bill Gates doesn't mind me asking, what the hell for?

Can my oven read? No. Does my oven have opposable thumbs? No, I have never caught my oven in the act of holding measuring spoons or assembling a cup of flour. Maybe I'm misunderstanding Gates's dreams for the future. Maybe he also plans to develop a smart oven with thumbs. That way, oh bless the gods, I can come home from work and have an oven-ready meal, prepared lovingly for me by a large appliance.

Did I mention what the hell for?

What's wrong with lifting frozen lasagna out of the freezer and sticking it in the oven myself? Am I so strapped for time, so physically enfeebled, that I can't even transfer objects from one appliance to another?

What all this amounts to is a perfect encapsulation of the tizzy that the information technology revolution has got itself in. As I see it, the world divides into two groups: There are those who, like Bill Gates, are nine-year-old boys at heart, saying, "Wouldn't it be cool if we could attach giant springs to our feet, so all we had to do to get to school would be to jump off the roofs of our houses and land in the homeroom in one *bounce*?" And those who reply: "Not really, no."

Belonging to this second group, I am cringing at the thought of the impending, home-based software revolution. What do I need in my kitchen and bathroom that isn't there already? Did I need an electric toothbrush? Did I require a K-Tel automatic hamburger patty stacker? Do I sit around pining for one of those things that instantly seals plastic bags? Have I ever once used more than ten percent of the available functions on my VCR remote control? I'm still figuring out the efficacy of household technologies from the 1970s, like the butter temperature switch in my fridge, which never seems to have the faintest impact on the relative solidity of my butter even though I occasionally change it, out of curiosity, from "medium" to "soft."

My mother-in-law, an inveterate watcher of infomercials, once acquired a remote-control camping lantern, which could be turned on and off from twenty yards away. Somehow this eased her anxiety about what might happen if, at the age of seventy-eight, she suddenly needed to sleep in a tent in the woods and had to go to the bathroom and a fairy stole her flashlight while she was more than twenty yards from her sleeping bag . . . just as the sun set and plunged everything into darkness.

At least she didn't have to upgrade the technology on her never-used lantern. I, on the other hand, buy a perfectly useful computer and discover that its parts are obsolete within twelve months because the "*wouldn't it be great?*" crowd are at the helm of computer companies. My office has become not so much a graveyard for electronics as an orphanage. I have three computers in my closet that I was simply forced to abandon when I discovered that their makers would no longer supply me with replacement batteries. There are entire cars out there on the road putt-putting around that are older than my parents, and I can't keep a computer operating for longer than the shelf-life of cold medicine.

God forbid that anyone should still own a tape deck or a VCR. When DVDs began slinking onto the shelves at my local Blockbuster, just innocently presenting themselves in unthreatening clusters beside the videos, my heart sank as I fingered the change in my pocket. How long, I wondered sadly, how long until I had to buy a DVD player in order to see movies? How long until I had to throw out all my cassettes because no car I rented would play anything but CDs?

There is a shift, I feel, and a wildly disconcerting one, between the days of being asked by wildly hopeful advertisers to buy stupid things on late-night TV and a market that *makes* you spend new money on products by undermining the value of what you have. The market, and the choices, are ever so slowly growing less free.

Let It All Come Down

Eight thirty at night and I've just received a call from Alba, who works for a credit card company.

"Patricia," she ventured, in a soft and almost tentative voice, "I'm concerned that you haven't made your minimum payment this month, is everything all right?"

I pulled the phone away from my ear and stared at it in puzzled disgust. The tone of her question was so intimate and so worried that I imagined her asking for an update on my marriage.

Are you all right? Have robbers stolen your wallet? Did a tornado whirl through your house? Is there anything I can do?

"Oh. Right," I said. "I'll pay right away."

And I did. The next day I mailed a cheque. But still I received two more phone calls in as many days inquiring about my personal state of mental health. By the weekend I lay in bed imagining the conversation I really ought to have had with Alba.

"I hesitate to be rude, Alba," I should have said, twirling the phone cord between my fingers as I felt my pulse speed up, priming for the challenge, "but I feel like maybe

you're behaving a bit oddly. Has that occurred to you?
Do you not think it's odd to phone someone at home, at
night, whom you have never met, and inquire about her
personal mental health? Is it possible that you don't feel
concern for me so much as for your job, which would at
least render your concern plausible? Is it okay for me to
say that? Is your job at risk if I don't pay my minimum
payment? Like, are you on a minimum-payment commission or something? I could phone your manager and
explain that you and I are concerned about each other
and that we are going to work this out privately. I could
say, 'Back off, this is between me and Alba.'"

I imagined her falling silent for a time, and then stonily
falling back upon her point: "It would be helpful if you
made a payment."

"Okay, Alba," I would say, sadly and reflectively. "Okay."

I actually have no objection to paying my bills, although
I sometimes forget for a while. What alarms me, however,
is the sequence of behaviours that credit card companies
engage in as they transform you from potential client to
serf. Is it not slightly creepy? At first, they court you aggressively. The other day, for instance, I was writing about being
driven daft by consumer choices, when the phone rang,
and incautiously I dared to answer it. Without further ado,
I found myself listening to an impenetrable monologue
from a department store sales rep about some sort of insurance plan that could be applied to my card *right now*, this
minute, provided I digested everything he was babbling
about on the spot, whereupon all I had to do was say "yes."

"But I have absolutely no idea what you're talking about," I pointed out. "Can't you just send me something in the mail?"

"No ma'am, this offer is only available now, bla de bla." And off he went again, explaining something that I had neither the time nor the patience to deconstruct, while the pleasant task of . . . well . . . damning hucksters just like him swiftly faded and I had to take a break. Go to my corner Starbucks. Order a no-whip, decaf, grande mocha latte with a shot of Thorazine. Dream of escape.

Came home to find credit cards flinging themselves through my mail slot with offers of preapproved cards and extravagant compliments about my special status as a recipient. A friend's four-year-old son was preapproved for one of these cards, which we thought was interesting, given that all he would think to do was use the card as a diving board for his Rescue Heroes.

Essentially, these are cards that you would otherwise never think to apply for—because you're fine. Doing fine. But after ignoring eighteen that come through the mail, you look at the nineteenth and start to think, Wow. Seven thousand dollars' credit preapproved! Consider how much microwave popcorn, Primordiale Nuit lotion, and funerals you could buy!

Ah, what the hell. You get the card. The low interest rate strings you along for a while until it evaporates and you're laying out roughly twelve times the bank rate in interest just to pay off new shoes. Hello, quagmire of debt. Then, this is what credit card companies do. They dog you with their weird pseudo-intimate inquiries when you find yourself a week past due. It's scary, because this does not happen with the phone company or the furnace guys. They send you reminder notices in the mail, and then eventually just threaten to cut you off. They don't pretend they care. And thus, they don't betray you in the way that credit card companies do when you still fail to pay, for whatever reason, and the nicey-nice credit card people drop the temperature in their voices to frigid and kneecap you with a baseball bat.

I know this, because in the space of six weeks, one memorable time, I moved houses and gave birth to a son, with the predictable result that I entirely forgot about a rarely used credit card whose minimal billings no longer arrived at the correct address. Busy as I was, swaying back and forth and back and forth to Bob Marley tunes as Geoffrey bawled in his Snugli, I was taken off guard one day by a phone call from a "Mr. Hobbs." He left a number but no explanation as to why he had called.

Unlike Alba, who didn't give me her last name, Mr. Hobbs refused to give me his first name, when I got back to him, in a spirit of perfect reversal. Alba was my friend. Mr. Hobbs was not. He informed me that I owed the full bill to this credit card company immediately, and then he told me to phone him back when I had made payment. I took note, scrawled out a cheque, and then resumed sleep deprivation and reggae staggering, planning to mail out a bunch of stuff on Friday. But, earth to new mother Patricia! No, no, no! Once you are in Hobbsian hands, you cannot wait until *Friday*. What are you, a freak? Less than twenty-four hours elapsed between our initial conversation and the time that Mr. Hobbs felt free to leave a message at Ambrose's office, pretending that he needed to reach me urgently and could not get through. At the same time, he went after Doug.

Doug.

Doug was my neighbour, a morgue technician at a nearby hospital who spent hours in his garage at night listening to Aerosmith and Led Zeppelin and tinkering with his proudly acquired second-hand Jaguar. Doug—he of the pale green scrubs—had a preternatural George Hamilton tan, a receding hairline, and two boisterous blond sons who played road hockey in the alley. He also had a wife—a lean, curly-haired woman named April who was constantly and tensely engaged in the weeding and pruning of her postage-stamp garden.

"Oh, for God's sake," April would mutter loudly on her side of the fence, knowing that I was on the other side, "I am so sick of this."

I was left to presume that she meant my cats, who were probably pooing in her trowelled rows of compost, but she wasn't the sort to say it directly, just glared at me whenever we chanced to see each other over the ivy.

I never saw April and Doug at the neighbourhood cafés and bars or the chic shops that lined our street. They shunned the funky downtown core in which they were inescapably trapped by the convenient walk to their hospital jobs, and their unhappiness was palpable, and toxic. The day that Mr. Hobbs saw fit to call Ambrose's workplace, Doug came over and twisted our old-fashioned doorbell.

"Hi," he said, staring wildly over my head and using a tone that barked *I am not interested in you or your phone calls*, "I got a message for you to call someone named Mr. Hobbs." He handed me the phone number.

I gaped in astonishment. "That is bizarre!" I exclaimed. Then I asked, as an afterthought, "Did Mr. Hobbs phone you today?"

Maybe this was from before Hobbs had reached me, I thought, maybe he was not deliberately trying to portray me as a delinquent slut unfit for the neighbourhood, while shaming me at the same time in front of my husband's work colleagues. Maybe . . . ?

Doug nodded. Today. He still wouldn't make eye contact. I understood that it was part of Doug's tangled and water-logged fate to share this neighbourhood with writers and artists and Vietnamese people when he was, simply, Doug. He just wanted everyone to go away. His wife, with her brittle snip-snapping about not stepping on the tulips, his bouncy children, the dead bodies, the breast-feeding neighbours with collection agents on their case. As I perceived it, Doug wanted to relive the successful part of his life that had taken place in a garage somewhere with Aerosmith and a car. Over and over, he wanted this, like the movie *Groundhog Day*, but played out as a fantasy rather than a cautionary tale.

I took the number, thanked Doug, and retreated inside. I phoned Mr. Hobbs and flared with outrage that he had done what he'd done. Was he insane? Had the rules of civilized conduct changed? Mr. Hobbs calmly passed me over to his manager, pro forma. You could tell he did it all the time. And as God, the sleeping Geoffrey, and Ambrose are my witnesses, this woman, his manager, dressed me down with such fervour and vitriol that I felt like a suspect in serial homicide.

"Don't you ever, EVER, talk to one of my employees that way," she bellowed.

"Your employee called my neighbour!" I protested.

"My employees are professionals who do whatever is required to make people like you honour your outstanding debts." People like me. I was a mother in a bathrobe and detachable bra flaps.

"You are to MARCH down to the nearest Money Mart," she commanded, "do you understand? And WIRE the entire amount that you owe, RIGHT NOW."

I tried to argue with her, but she interrupted me with verbal thumps against my chest. "Do you want to go to JAIL? Is that it? Do you want to go to JAIL?"

Berated and screamed at until I finally capitulated, I left the baby with Ambrose and obediently went off to wire the full amount I owed to the collection agency from a nearby Money Mart, only later confirming that nothing like that—NOTHING—was mandated under Ontario law. You do, in fact, get to send a cheque by snail mail. You do not, in fact, face the prospect of imprisonment for doing so.

I have never hated anyone in my entire life as vehemently

as I hated Mr. Hobbs and his army-issue boss. For weeks I plotted my revenge, à la Uma Thurman in *Kill Bill*. But ultimately, there was very little that I could do, other than file a complaint with the relevant government ministry. Instead, I signed up for a course, entitled "How to Hide Your Assets and Disappear."

It's not the government you need to worry about in terms of invasion of privacy, the instructor said, it's the private sector. Just so.

CONSOLATIONS FOR THE NEUROTIC MODERN PARENT

Shakespeare's Nanny

When my son was eleven months old, the question arose: How do I get somebody else to stand around, stupefied with boredom, while he drops a rubber duck into the toilet, fishes it out, drops it in, fishes it out, cries, spies a stray bit of Kleenex, drops that in, discovers that it has disintegrated, cries? In other words, I wanted to go back to work.

Do I pack him off to daycare as I did my daughter, or do I hire some sort of nanny, preferably one who, through a rare genetic disorder affecting the cerebral cortex, cannot be judgmental about the catastrophic state of my house?

Nothing in the world makes women more insanely neurotic than having a nanny. It doesn't matter who the nanny is. She could be Mother Teresa, in which case the mother would start worrying that her nanny was more concerned about world poverty than toddler gymnastics. What if, as a result of Nanny Teresa's neglect, baby Jimmy grew up to be uncoordinated? What then? As soon as a woman hires a nanny, she's off and running with outlandish paranoia. One of my sanest friends recently confided in me that she thought her nanny was putting poison in her son's Cheerios.

"Whaddya mean—like rat poison?"

"Yeah, I'm not kidding. He's been getting really sick after breakfast."

"Correct me if I'm wrong, but didn't you think that your last nanny was slipping him Quaaludes?"

"Yes, but that was just a misunderstanding. This is different. I think she has a lot of repressed hostility."

There is no reasonable response to this kind of frenzied maternal fretting jag, and I've heard it so many times that it makes me lean toward daycare. There's the occasional Satanic abuse worry at daycares, of course, but for the most part mothers don't tend to get into weird psychotic turf wars with daycare staffers. Instead, they just feel guilty. Guilty, guilty, guilty, alllll the time. "Bye sweetie, I'm just dropping you off here—please stop screaming and clutching my leg— because it's important that I permanently undermine our attachment and warp your development, according to several new studies, and also MUMMY HAS TO GO TO WORK NOW, PLEASE LET GO OF MY PANTS."

I try to follow the daycare vs. Mommy debates, but the logic seems to travel in small vicious circles. At some point you get to wondering: Well, what is seriously going to happen if my children go to daycare, or have a nanny? Like, are they going to become contract killers, or are they going to be somewhat more argumentative in adolescence? Exactly *how* damaged a future are the experts envisioning as a result of substitute care? This led me to think about the child care arrangements of history's most accomplished men and women. Maybe history could frame the debate a little more concisely. For instance, did Shakespeare have a nanny? Because if he did, then, end of conversation, as far as I'm concerned.

So I perused a few biographies in the local bookstore, and here are my preliminary notes:

Elizabeth I, Queen of England: When a toddler, mother's head chopped off. Spent childhood locked in Tower of London. Perhaps had some attachment issues later on, but nevertheless became greatest ruler of England ever. (Studies show that thinking of oneself as a semi-divine being can often compensate for decapitated or working mother.)

Jane Austen, romantic novelist: Sent by parents to pass infant and toddler years in a hut, being raised by peasants until parents deemed child "more interesting." Child became so interesting she invented Mr. Darcy, upon whom all twenty-first-century women now have crush.

Peter the Great, Tsar of Russia: Raised by staff of fourteen dwarfs. Admittedly, was rather boorish as grown-up but had a good time and managed to modernize Russia. Important to know: Was there high staff turnover among the dwarfs, or were they always the same fourteen, ensuring constancy of care?

Michelangelo, painter of the Sistine Chapel: Wealthy parents putter about country estate near Florence while baby lives with wet nurse in shed. Mother becomes muse for *La Pietà* and is thus immortalized rather than made to answer questions about how could she put her own interests ahead of her child's crucial early development.

Katharine Graham, publisher of the *Washington Post*: As infant, left with nanny in a Fifth Avenue flat while parents moved to Washington for four years. As adult, finally follows them to the capital—with a vengeance.

Thomas Jefferson: Raised by clinically depressed slaves. Daughters also raised by slaves. One slave becomes mother of youngest son, who therefore becomes slave. Life confusing, but very productive.

Sleeping Beauties

I love my children, but my life would be much improved if they were unconscious more often. Ideally, my four-year-old could go to sleep at six, say, and then wake up at ten the next morning. Or if that's too ambitious, what if it got to be eight-thirty P.M. and she scrambled into bed and closed her eyes, instead of climbing onto the kitchen table and drawing on her legs with a pen?

Still too aspiring? Then maybe she could just fall asleep before I do.

Conversely, my baby son could try sleeping until it was light outside in the morning, because it was fine to watch the Athens Olympics live, but on the whole I would rather not have one child fall asleep at eleven and the other one wake up at five.

Every time Ambrose and I go on a "date," the fun is overshadowed by the dread of getting to bed too late and being dragged to our feet before dawn with a hangover stunningly magnified by sleep deprivation.

We keep hoping, instead, to spend time with each other privately at home, which is like waiting for Godot. When

Ambrose kissed me recently in front of Clara, she cried out in genuine astonishment: "What are you doing?" Oh, never mind. We resumed staring gloomily at our children not-sleeping.

The children beam back like little rays of sunshine; life's a never-ending bed-bouncing blast when you're small. Bedtime? Yay! Time for back flips, giggling fits, five trips to the bathroom, three to the fridge, and then sixteen outfit changes. Yippee!

In the la-la-land inhabited by experts in parenting books, Mommy serenely reads bedtime stories, sings songs, and rubs the child's back in a comforting ritual that leads smoothly to sleep. In my land, serene Mommy turns very gradually into serial killer Mommy, after reading, singing, and rubbing culminates in child hopping gaily out of bed.

Sleepy child flies downstairs to get her Barbie/ballet slippers/half-eaten banana before returning to discourse vigorously on who is and is not invited to her birthday party in two months' time.

Serene Mommy screams "GET INTO BED RIGHT NOW!" And sleepy child looks totally shocked, before bursting into tears and wailing "DAAAADDDDYY!" At which point, serene Mommy kvetches, "Daddy has nothing to do with this!" feeling bitter that her authority is so swiftly undercut by the prospect of divine rescuing Daddy.

Serene Mommy points out churlishly that Daddy, a.k.a. God, is lying in a stupor in the other room, after having swayed the baby back and forth to Bob Marley tunes for several hours. Sleepy child proceeds to fling *Guess How Much I Love You* off the bed.

At ten-thirty, sleepy child is finally sleepy and wishing to snuggle, and serene Mommy is so stiff with suppressed rage that she's about as snuggly as particle board.

So it goes, with minor variations, no thanks to the smug advice of other parents who consider themselves towering founts of wisdom because their children happen to be biddable. "I find," a typical parent chimes helpfully, "that after I read angel three stories, I tell her that Mommy's just going downstairs to make tea, and when I come back she's asleep."

Well, I don't find that, do I? I find that angel follows me downstairs and asks for a dish of noodles.

Of course, where I see a problem, entrepreneurs see an opportunity, so I note that there's a burgeoning crop of GO TO SLEEP audio products on the market. Video producer Kandi Amelon in Chicago, for instance, has recently released *Nighty Night*, a twenty-minute cinematic extravaganza of yawning baby animals, courtesy of Peter Pan Productions.

In my view, this is designed to induce sleep through boredom, whereas the more traditional videos, like *Sweet Dreams, Spot*, and *Maisy's Bedtime*, merely hint at the popularity of sleep among a child's favourite characters, much the way that every preschool book ever published ends with the hero comatose in a bed.

Videos are not the answer in this house, because there's something creepy and Brave New World about having electronic portals in every bedroom.

I prefer cassettes. Since Clara spent the first six months of her life listening to a continuous loop recording of vacuum cleaner noise, there's cause for hope.

Thus I found *The Floppy Sleep Game* tape, created by a cheerful California lady named Patti Teel. A children's entertainer in Burbank, Teel has been garnering great word of mouth for the "progressive relaxation technique" she's adapted from yoga and embedded in her game. Hyper children are said to be snoozing within half an hour, after listening to her Betty Boop voice direct them in a sort of self-hypnosis exercise.

I ordered the tape, and excitedly played it for Clara when all other rituals had been attended to. She was sitting cross-legged on her bed, avidly popping the bubbles from a padded envelope.

Teel's voice materialized in a tinkle of music and encouraged her to lie down. Clara obliged, holding the envelope above her to resume popping. To the faint sound of crickets, Teel said: "Close your eyes, and imagine that you're lying outside on a blanket in your own, special meadow."

Clara continued popping. "You're supposed to close your eyes," I prompted.

"Why?"

"Because we're playing the floppy sleep game."

"What does floppy mean?"

"It means . . . I don't know, like . . . a rag doll."

"What's a rag?"

"It's an old washcloth, Clara—just listen to the tape."

"Lift your leg and let it flop down again," murmured Teel. Clara engaged in the body relaxation instructions for a while, then went back to her bubble popping. When Teel segued into a lullaby, Clara deconstructed the lyrics like Jacques Derrida.

"Oh, forget it," I muttered, turning the tape recorder off.

"Mommy? Are you tired?"

"Yes, as a matter of fact, I am."

"You can go to sleep if you want to."

Oh, thanks.

Last night I had a dream about Benicio Del Toro, the actor who, being male, gets to stride around with puffy eyes, unwashed hair, and minimal makeup and still be considered THE most gorgeous specimen of Latin masculinity ever to emerge from small-town Pennsylvania. In my dream we were having a wonderful, wonderful romance, although for some reason we were in a dental office and I kept having to spit into a paper cup. But it was delicious and enthralling. When I woke up, Clara was feeding Chiclets to the cat.

Is That a Cheerio Stuck to My Pants, or Are You Just Happy to See Me?

I was at the Children's Museum with thousands of highly excited toddlers streaking by me in every direction like a huge colony of snowsuited ants, when at some point, feeling harried and claustrophobic, I looked up and noticed a dad checking me out.

No way! He can't be looking at me, can he? I'm a mom! What's he looking at? Is there something on my shirt? An unusually large smear of applesauce or snot? Because he can't be looking at *me*. I. Am. A. Mom. There must be Scotch tape on my pants.

Five years ago I might have registered his gaze as admiring or desirous or lustful, and it wouldn't have been rocket science. But here in the altered state of consciousness called motherhood, male attention inspires a slow-motion double take. I think it has to do with defining myself in the eyes of my children. My face could be a boiled ham, as far as they're concerned. Therefore, wondering if I look sexy is irrelevant, not to mention hopeless and entirely beside the point.

My sexuality has gone AWOL.

I cannot find it under the couch with the stray puzzle pieces and empty formula bottles. I cannot find it in the bathtub among the spouting whales and duckies. It isn't in the bedroom, which is knee-deep in Barbie shoes and crackers. Sometimes I wonder: Is my sexuality behind the garden gate in Geoffrey's lift-the-flap book? No, but there's Spot the dog and Tom, the green alligator, playing ball, yay! Is it in the refrigerator? No, but there are some crinkly grapes in there.

Surprisingly, I am married. This used to have a romantic connotation. I keep assuring myself, as Ambrose does, that all will be romantic again just as soon as we can reach for each other in a bed and not bump into two children, a Groovy Girl doll, the TV remote, our dog, a pacifier, and *Goodnight Moon*.

Wishing to be guaranteed of this eventuality, I recently attended a conference on motherhood, sex, and sexuality. The conference was organized by ARM, the Association for Research on Mothering, together with the Centre for Feminist Research. Much of the conversation centred on society's discomfort with maternal sexuality, but that attitude has actually grown more ambivalent of late. If we used to divide neatly into madonnas and whores and crones and virgins, what of the pop star Madonna, sauntering about on her book tours looking gorgeous in her forties with two children in tow?

She rather confounds the categories. But she works at it. Women are generally becoming mothers later now, in their thirties, when their sexual ambitions have played out a bit, seeds have been sown, blocks have been run around. We *were* whores, so to speak, and now too many of us are behaving like madonnas with chronic fatigue syndrome.

There's something the matter with that, which has to do with yielding to the loss of sexual vitality without a fight, as if it doesn't matter as much as it does. But maybe one of the reasons that we yield to the shift from sexy hottie to frumpy hen is that we derive a great deal of sensual nourishment from our small children.

This subject was explored rather intriguingly by one Pamela Courtney-Hall, a professor at the University of British Columbia. She proposed that many parents derive an erotic pleasure from their children that calls for a new vocabulary of sexuality or Eros, for it isn't sexual in the orthodox sense but deeply intimate and physically sustaining.

We declare child care to be an "Eros-neutral domain," Courtney-Hall said, "but caregivers report connections to their children that are rapturous . . . and rooted in intimate bodily contact." They are not sexual, however, not dirty and self-pleasuring, not pedophiliac. "The language we have inherited," she noted, "is inadequate to the lived experience."

Thus, mothers who unexpectedly find breastfeeding to be sensually enthralling are suspected of sexual abuse, while mothers who find their children's bodies beguiling, like the photographer Sally Mann, are accused of taking pornographic pictures.

This same point, about the unspoken "tender-erotic"

connection between parents and children, as Courtney-Hall calls it, is raised in a book by American writer Noelle Oxenhandler, *The Eros of Parenthood: Explorations in Light and Dark*. Oxenhandler tries to promote an invisible but uncrossable line between parental passion and pedophiliac lust, sensual joy and sexual exploitation. It's tricky and fraught, like playing with a conceptual hand grenade. I think most parents intuitively understand what's being spoken of without needing a language that can be so dangerously appropriated.

A child's bodily integrity is not at stake in a mother's embrace, but that doesn't mean that hugging your daughter is the same as hugging a friend. It is more intense and lovely and delicious. It also ends—at about the point when daughters make mothers walk five paces behind them in public so as not to be embarrassed in front of their friends.

Then it is probably time for a midlife crisis. Not the best path to tread, this celebration of the tender-erotic. Better—surely?—to insist upon our sexual vibrancy as women all along, to allow ourselves to be viewed as Madonna rather than as madonnas, as, if anything, more beautiful because of motherhood. I deserve to recognize a man's gaze in a crowded kid's museum for what it is, admiring, and take some sustenance from that.

Penises and Pryin' Eyes

I was sitting at the marina near my old cottage last summer, dumbly engrossed in a novel, when a woman came up to me and declared with great umbrage: "He is *pee*ing in the LAKE."

I looked up slowly—the way you do when it dawns on you that the ambient sound of someone blurting gibberish is actually addressed to you personally—and saw a sixtyish woman with smoker's wrinkles, sporting hot pants and carrying a dachshund, staring down at me and smiling very tightly.

"Oh, I'm sorry," I said, uncertainly. I assumed that she was referring to my dog. It is a well-known fact in North America that dogs can relieve themselves only in the one place—parks—where people like to sit, picnic, and go barefoot, usually slipping on smears of dog shit. Otherwise, dogs' needs are a constant embarrassment to the owner, as the dogs heedlessly urinate in lakes, on marigolds, against car tires and recycling boxes, into leaf piles, and alongside hedges belonging to cat owners. God forbid that dogs should defecate on the ground when you don't have a bag, because then you just have to perish from self-consciousness on the spot. It's the rule.

I readied myself to argue with this hectoring woman, but then I suddenly remembered that I didn't have my dog with me at the marina. Confused, I followed the limp, disdainful wave of her arm as she pointed across the docks, and realized that she was talking about my *son*.

Ohhhh, I nodded. Right. There was my son, naked, as is his wont, ever since he was busted loose from diapers and snow pants and the restrictions of the city. He was playing on a strip of sand near some boats and had evidently just executed an exciting arc of piss into the shallows.

I smiled apologetically. "Accidents happen at that age, you know. He doesn't always remember to come to me in time."

Of course, I knew that Geoffrey had peed in the lake deliberately, bending his knees and thrusting his pelvis forward in great I-love-my-penis glee, because that is what he's into these halcyon days of summer, and I don't care. Male friends have murmured admiringly to me about Geoffrey's penis-waggling because they were taught shame. If only they had had a bookish absent-minded mother who found nudity easier to deal with, frankly, than chasing a boy around and around the house attempting to clothe him, they tell me. Imagine their sexual confidence then!

If truth be told, I wasn't aware of this masculine evolution of the self, but still I intuitively agreed with my friends. I think Geoffrey's innocent happiness about his penis-gadget is touching and amusing to watch. But not so. The woman's prim, perturbed expression suggested that my explanation had not appeased her. "He needs to be in a diaper," she said.

"I can't put him in a diaper," I protested, aroused. "He's over three years old."

"Then make him wear a swimsuit," she countered.

Now my faced flushed. I put my novel down and got to my feet. "Are you suggesting that small children in swimsuits don't pee in the lake? You don't think your granddaughter pees in the lake through her swimsuit? Or are you telling me that Geoffrey shouldn't be naked?"

She drew her panting dachshund in closer to her chest, as if to protect him from my sudden hostility, and whipped out the proverbial feminine pistol: "It is the consensus here at the marina that your child should be clothed."

Errrgh. I so deeply hate that. I'm being discussed! I'm the subject of an impromptu town hall meeting! Over the Skittles and Aero bars at the cashier's counter in the store! I must go, now, to Peshawar on a mule.

"So you've been gossiping," I observed.

At this, she absolutely bridled. "I do not gossip," she vowed, as if I'd accused her of having sex with a goat.

Okay, so what was it then, her shared conversation, that came to its decisive consensus about the affront of Geoffrey's nudity? A matter of "what is to be done?" It had nothing in common with the savage dog that's been mauling children in the township, or the drug addict who has been stealing cash, or whether to intervene when a parent is seen cuffing her child with an appalling backhanded blow.

The quandary here was a naked toddler occasionally arriving at the marina in a boat, and this woman, I sensed, had seized the opportunity to forward her agenda when she saw Geoffrey flaunting the implications of nudity by peeing in the lake.

I gazed at her and shrugged helplessly. "You have your opinion," I said, "and I have mine."

But it didn't end there because I was left to deal with the issue of community relations. I have been spending summers at this lake since I was a baby. I was married here. My aunts and uncles and cousins and second cousins are scattered all around its shore.

To ignore the marina store gossip would be to make an anti-social statement, the sort of broad hit of contempt that is notable in a small community, where the reverberations of every comment and shift of mood are observed.

It isn't like the city, where anonymity presides and thus a kind of tolerance for everything but dog shit is assumed; that very weekend, gays from all over North America were getting married at Toronto city hall and celebrating Gay Pride Day, and here I was in that general vicinity discovering that the phrase "it just isn't done" still has currency.

Oh dear. I didn't want to give in to the communal consensus that nakedness in a boy of three isn't done.

"I have an idea," Ambrose later ventured. "Why don't we come back to the marina with Geoffrey fully clothed, and me naked?"

I loved that idea; I thrilled to it and laughed. But in

the end he chickened out, didn't he? Because he was a man who had been a boy when it just wasn't done.

"Here's the deal," I said to Geoffrey when I'd given it some thought. "I want you to wear underwear, because you're going to spill hot soup on that penis of yours or fall down and scrape it, and you need to protect yourself, okay?"

From a motherlode of fear about male sexuality, and those pryin' affronted eyes.

My Lousy Job

If, as a working parent, you wish to be stopped in your tracks for ten days, I highly recommend a lice infestation in your children's hair. There is simply nothing that even comes close to ruining your status as an efficient office worker like being unable to find the *last one* of eleven thousand seven hundred and twenty nits the size of dust molecules on a six-year-old's head.

In my case, the whole fiasco of lice began with me, myself, walking around with an itchy scalp for about two weeks, thinking that I really ought to do a hot oil treatment in this very dry weather. Given that I shampoo every day and wear fashion mousse, it never occurred to me that I had insects nesting on my head.

Instead, naturally, it was the schoolteacher who discovered the lice crawling through my daughter's ponytail because only schoolteachers can see lice. It's part of their training in teacher's college, to be able to spot minuscule species of insects from ten feet across the room and then cry out a special code blue that all of the other teachers hear and respond to.

If there has been sensitivity training around the whole issue of lice—they're not caused by Dickensian living conditions, Mother is not necessarily an alcoholic, etc.— I cannot vouchsafe that this training has worked. The school called me and commanded that I pick up my children AS SOON AS POSSIBLE, regardless of whether I was just then in the process of selling London's *Daily Telegraph* to the Barclay Brothers, or conducting surgery, so that none of the other, better-tended and hygienic children would get cooties.

Then, when I arrived, out of breath and apologetic, the teacher reassured me that lice were really no big deal; a special shampoo would do the trick and everyone could get back to business. This left me with the false impression that I was contending with a mere twenty-four-hour emergency.

I collected the children and went directly to the pharmacy to find the special shampoo. When I went home and applied it, I discovered that it kills, maybe, one louse and has no impact whatsoever on the nits. It does not take twenty-four hours to remove that many nits from two little heads, because neither head will keep still for longer than thirty seconds unless they are clamped in an iron vise.

Use of a vise is not possible, given the interest it tends to attract from the Children's Aid Society. So I had to plead with my children, cajole them, yell at them, chase them around the house, threaten them with a total moratorium on toy purchases, bribe them with more toys than they could ever play with, and finally sit on them while they shook their heads wildly and wailed, "We will never surrender!"

Unless you have dealt with nit capture, you have no idea how impossible it is to remove one nit if the host head moves more than one one-millionth of a centimetre in any direction before you have grasped it.

Clara eventually grew somewhat compliant for stretches of five or six minutes, but Geoffrey is a three-year-old. The merest whisper of a suggestion of obedience leads to freaked-out shrieks of counter-suggestion, and it becomes a matter of psychologically-developmental necessity for him to refuse to allow me to remove insects from his head. Nor would stealth work. He could detect the approach of my hovering nit comb with the acuity of a fly on the windowsill and get away just in time.

Finally, I had to wait for them to fall asleep so that I could root around on their heads in the darkness like a deranged jewel thief, with me nit-picking as Ambrose aimed the flashlight. Lice, however, have evolved the ability to be invisible in all but the brightest noon-time light when only a teacher can see them. We would think that we'd conquered them in our nocturnal attacks, only to realize next morning that we'd nabbed less than half.

Thus, the children were boomeranged back at us when we meekly attempted to resubmit them to class, with the staff practically holding crucifixes aloft and sprinkling holy water in their bouncy, retreating tracks. Growing desperate, we slathered their heads in condiments, at the suggestion of cheerful "no problema" friends. My daughter sported mayonnaise for several hours, and my son slept in a cap of olive oil. Furniture and carpets were doused in vinegar. Everything emerged smelling odd and looking shiny. Within a week the nits were back.

You will never hear this confession in congressional testimony or from a mother being interviewed on Larry King, but the truth is this: I had my son's head shaved in order to resume my career.

Almost-Forgotten Rites of Passage

The week that Clara entered grade one, the *New Yorker* featured a cartoon depicting two mothers on a park bench watching their toddlers at play. One mother was remarking glumly to the other: "They grow up so slow."

Oh yes, I get that. Every parent who just spent Labour Day weekend with a three-year-old and a six-year-old screaming at each other about who "gets to poke the dead fish" can relate to that sentiment.

Time flows as slowly as molasses when you have to spend it trying and failing to get a sun hat on a toddler, or trying and failing to get your six-year-old to under-stand that God and Santa Claus are NOT the only ones who get to make the rules.

"Go to bed."

"No."

"You have to go to bed because it's the first day of school tomorrow."

"You don't make the rules."

"Yes, I do."

"Only God and Santa—"

"GO TO BED."

Aaargh.

Yet mothers of older children adamantly argue the opposite point: "No! No!" they cry in alarm. "Kids don't grow up slow; they grow up FAST." Indeed, such parents hammer this into my head at every opportunity, as if all will be lost if I don't grasp what they are trying to say. But what *are* they trying to say? What lies at the root of this parental perception of time-warp? It doesn't seem to apply to one's spouse or parent or pet. Nobody ever says to me, "Oh my God, my husband is aging so fast!"

It isn't a perception of time flying, but something else. I wonder if it's about control—that you lose control of your children faster than you anticipated that you would. Do you slip from the centre to the periphery of their universe before you're prepared to, before you've taught them everything you wanted them to know? There is always a sense of regret affixed to the notion of children growing up fast, a feeling that one is caught off-guard because one wasn't watching.

Whatever it is that is lost, the universally acknowledged threshold for a child's crossing into the speedier time zone is grade one. Baby goes to school. There is so much hype around this entry point that the occasion is made momentous. It would be unthinkably crass to send one's child with the nanny, or a friend, to the first day of grade one. Pictures must be taken. Sunday-best outfits donned.

All this hype and all the sentiments were very much on my mind yesterday when my daughter and I crossed that threshold together. There were only two problems. The first was that as a working mother who rushes from one daily crisis to another, grade one kind of snuck up on me. I had it written down in my daybook, so to speak, but I hadn't thought over what it entailed.

Thus at midnight on Labour Day I realized that I had no idea what time school started: Eight-thirty? Eight-forty-five? Nine? Oh, God.

And what was Clara supposed to bring? A pencil? Some gym clothes? And where was she going to have lunch?

So I rose at dawn on the Big Day and flew around the house in a neurotic fluster. I hastily did her laundry, assembled random school-like contents for her knapsack, and tried hurriedly to find a "bread substitute" for her lunch sandwich since I hadn't thought to get any groceries.

"You're such a loser," I scolded myself as I stuffed her lunch box full of leftover barbecued salmon and Cheetos.

We got out the door at eight-fifteen. "Am I late for school?" Clara asked, as we trotted along the sidewalk.

"I don't know," I muttered. "I hope not."

Au contraire, we were thirty-five minutes early. This gave me sufficient time to ponder the second problem, which was really more a dawning revelation. To wit: Times have changed. Grade one doesn't feel like that big a day.

Clara, you see, is a daycare child and I am a working mother. We were not dealing with our first full-time separation. I did not look at her with her knapsack and her new shoes, and think: "It seems like only yesterday that she was a babe in my arms bawling from colic." I didn't feel that pang of nostalgia. Clara has been beyond my control and among her peers since she was ten months old.

Clara stood comfortably in the crowded hall, yakking with friends, waving at her kindergarten teacher, showing off her Barbie bracelet. She knew what to do, in some ways, better than I did. She lined up expertly along the wall when the bell rang and then slid past me, smiling at her new teacher and scampering into the classroom without so much as a "seeya later."

"Oh," I said, still standing there. "Well, okay then . . ." I suppose I'll just go to work now.

I left the school with a good friend who had just deposited his daughter alongside mine. We fretted about the huge class size and wondered if our daughters would be all right eating their lunches in the gym. And then, as swiftly, we moved on to other topics—to our work lives, our marriages. At one point, I thought: "We should be talking about the Big Day more, shouldn't we? Isn't it momentous?" Then I shrugged and kept on walking. They grow up so slow, you think. And then one day you realize they're growing up just fine.

My Sunny Valentine

The other day Clara excitedly sang a song that she'd learned in her grade one classroom:

"Clara and Lucas sitting in a tree, K R M L B M G."

I started chuckling.

"Why are you laughing?" she asked, her sweet heart-shaped face lit up with concern. "What does the song mean?"

"You didn't get the letters quite right," I explained, "but they're supposed to spell out 'kissing.'"

"Oh," she said, smiling in surprise. But she still didn't get why the song would be salacious and meant to tease. I can't explain romantic love to a six-year-old, because it would be inseparable in her experience from familial love. She wants to grow up to marry her father, and everything else is merely idiom and play.

I was reminded of that yesterday when she overheard talk of Valentine's Day and asked me what it was for.

"Well," I started brightly, opting for a religious explanation, "it's a special day in honour of Saint Valentine, who . . . uh . . . er . . ." Of course, I couldn't remember who Saint

Valentine was. "Anyway, it's a day when you tell people that you love them."

"Why?"

Why being the classic follow-up question of all small children on every subject, guaranteeing that you gape like a carp while you try to formulate an elaborate response to an issue that you haven't thought about. Why don't we tell people that we love them on the other 364 days of the year? Hmmm, well, I guess we do, so . . . really it gets back to celebrating Saint Valentine, who was . . . er . . . oh, never mind. Finish your Cheerios.

Clara plays with weddings and family units and the idea of boyfriends, and last summer we were surprised to find her group playing spin the bottle in someone's basement, without having the faintest clue that the objective was the kiss, rather than the spinning of the bottle, which they all thought was very cool. But I watch her and wonder: When do children genuinely grasp the concept of romantic love? Do their parents see it coming? Are we prepared to take the revelation seriously after years of watching puppy-like rehearsals?

Shortly after our conversation, the local paper ran a story about this question as posed by Dr. Wendy Austin, a University of Alberta mental health expert who has written a book about early adolescent love. In *First Love: The Adolescent's Experience of Amour*, Austin argues that adults don't take teenaged infatuations as seriously as they should. Of course, it's difficult to take the matter seriously when your child's love is the two-dimensional image of a pop star on a poster or the son of your best friend, who you still remember being transfixed by Bob the Builder.

But Austin feels that adults misperceive how powerful their children's feelings are when they first develop a "crush" on someone, and because they don't understand, parents risk alienating their children by not being able to guide them through a hugely tempestuous experience.

I agree with this up to a point. But to judge from some articles and documentaries I've caught lately, it is teens themselves who are currently avoiding romance. Instead, they're just checking out sex. Fellatio in school bathrooms. "Hooking up" for quick screws rather than dating. Hanging out—not with their Romeos—but with guys that the girls call "friends with benefits." This news, I must confess, has a tendency to make me want to gnaw straight through the kitchen table and then contemplate where to send my daughter for safekeeping from twelve to twenty. Which nunnery? I don't remember caring whether or not my mother took seriously my love for the singer Cat Stevens, but if I'd been giving him oral sex in the stairwell with no promise of anything so much as a prom date in return, I think I would have wanted my mother to snap me out of it.

I certainly agree with Austin saying this: "We talk to young people about sexual health, but we don't really talk to them about love."

We talk to them about the beginnings of love, its early sweetness—if not explicitly, then through the fairy tales we read to them and the romantic Disney movies we bring home for them to watch, about Snow White, Pocahontas, Mulan, Sleeping Beauty, the Little Mermaid. But these happy stories scarcely rehearse them for love's danger. Never mind the unexpected miseries that overwhelm the cavalier heart. We let them play with fire without a warning. And far from maturing them or strengthening their independence, the sex that now goes hand in hand with anything resembling love renders them all the more vulnerable.

To give all of yourself, both symbolically and actually, to a fellow child who recklessly throws you over is an absolutely devastating experience, for which our culture shows little respect. I remember feeling deeply confused, in my early twenties, by the fact that a woman who was widowed or divorced received solemn recognition for the love that she lost, but I did not. I got dumped; I couldn't wear black. My love had less value. My heartbreak less meaning.

"To dismiss it as superficial, comical or trivial is to underestimate the power it has over the individual," notes Dr. Austin.

Alas, in our world, the length of time between first crush and anything approaching a ritual acknowledgement of love is growing longer and longer, as twelve-year-olds have sex and thirty-year-olds remain unmarried. Eighteen years of hoped-for valentines and broken hearts with no help in mending? Surely I must come up with an imaginative and caring way to prepare my little daughter for that.

The Seven Circles of Heck

I recently had an opportunity to tour the seesaws and beehives of Italy, which I highly recommend as a travel itinerary if you are (a) insane or (b) in the company of a toddler.

Travelling through Italy with a toddler is not hell, because the country is so divinely beautiful that even the many, many beetles that get pointed out by one's teensy tourist are gorgeous to look at. Albeit, they are buzzing around some humdrum playground in a village, forty-five minutes' drive from Florence, capital of the Renaissance, to which you dare not venture because your toddler will be creamed by a scooter in five seconds flat.

But still, if you combine the beauty of the Italian countryside with the unromantic tantrums of your offspring, you come up with an experience that feels less like hell than heck.

I am now going to face myself in the mirror and concede that I just spent several thousand dollars on a trip to heck.

Why did I do this? Well, before Clara was born, my

husband and I had lots of travel lust, and the spending power of gnats. We drove to Cape Breton once, and went into debt on the gas.

Then Clara came along and we took a journey into the Twilight Zone of infant colic, which was free, and after that a tentative foray to Florida, which resulted in the worst fight of our entire relationship, fuelled by the huge irritability of being trapped in a beachside motel with a teething baby.

So we were feeling rather unfulfilled in the realm of romantic adventure.

"I refuse to accept this," I told Ambrose. "I'm not going to drag around our neighbourhood encountering the same dull vistas over and over until I'm fifty."

Let's damn well go to Italy. I'll stand among the ruins and fantasize about Jude Law. (Of course I didn't say that out loud.)

I bought some guidebooks and began to plan. The first obstacle I encountered, from a mother's point of view, was Rome. I wanted to be in Rome, city of Fellini and Loren and Michelangelo and excellent sunglasses. But I couldn't figure out how to be in Rome with a toddler.

What's in Rome? Priceless art, crazed traffic, mad crowds, stray cats riddled with disease, gelato as an all-meal substitute. Who would be strolling with me through the gorgeous piazzas? A witless, zany loose cannon about eighteen inches high who would rather fling herself into the Trevi Fountain than be deprived of a fifth ice-cream cone.

Are guidebooks useful on this point? No, they are not.

In one sense Rome is the perfect place for toddlers, because it's the birthplace of opera. Operatic theatrics combined with indecipherable words—toddlers should write opera, I've always thought. The plot could go something like this:

Hero strides into the Coliseum and comes across a mangy, half-dead cat: "The kitty, the kitty, I want to pat the kitty!"

Hero's mother: "No, no! It's too daaaaangerous!"

Hero (streaking over to glowering animal): "But I must, I must, the gods have willed it!"

Hero's mother (grabbing him away in fear): "The kitty's not friendly!" Both wail in sorrow/anger: "NOOOO/ BUT I WANT TOOOOO."

Breast beating and hair pulling ensue. Et cetera.

We decided to stay in Capranica, a village forty kilometres north of Rome, where Clara could run around unencumbered on a hazelnut farm. Good plan. Gaze longingly at Rome from afar while small child mouths unripe nuts and poisonous mushrooms. This, of course, necessitated renting a car at Rome's Fiumicino airport. Very bad plan.

My husband to Hertz car rental guy, upon arrival at the airport: "Good morning, here's our prepaid voucher for one thousand dollars for the automatic car rental?"

Hertz guy (and here I paraphrase): "Ah yes, well thank you for the money, and have a nice time in Italy without your car, which we didn't bother to procure."

"You don't have an automatic?"

"No; but we liked your money very much, thank you, and have a nice holiday."

Three days, many hundred dollars, and one car rental later (from the efficient and courteous Maggiore), Hertz coughed up a Chevy Opel.

Good. Now it's time to get HOPELESSLY LOST on Italian roads for ten days with a small child in the back seat whose incipient tantrum can be sensed like a darkening funnel cloud. At least there was a frisson of suspense in our travelling: "Can we make it to the two-animal zoo in nearby Poppi before the thunder erupts? What's our contingency plan? A variety store in suburban Viterbo that definitely sells ice cream, for sure."

So it was that we motored around Lazio and Tuscany, making many wonderfully spontaneous stops in supermarkets, with the occasional bold strike into towns of actual note. Siena, for instance, where Clara found and ate a piece of chewed gum with a footprint in it.

We also managed Tivoli, the lovely hill town east of Rome where the Emperor Hadrian built his magnificent country palace. Hadrian's villa is a huge, rambling compound of evocative rubble rather like Rome's Palatine Hill. It can be toured with a toddler provided that the toddler agrees to stay in her stroller. Clara opted, instead, to conceal herself in a hedge.

One notion that springs to mind, now that I've toured the shrubbery of Hadrian's villa, is that ruins and ancient monuments require a daydreamy engagement on the part of the tourist. You need to enter into a kind of reverie, imagining the emperor and his retinue striding past the marble columns. But small children force you to be highly attuned to the present, pondering the whereabouts of nettles in the undergrowth, for example.

As a result, having no time to imagine the past, evocative rubble evokes very little, really. What you need, given how split your attention will be, is totally explicit, in-your-face culture.

In other words, you need to hang out in a city like Rome.

When we finally dared to drive into Rome, which involved getting lost on the infamous Grande Autostrada circling the city and being obliged to consult with two transsexuals in a bowling alley, we began to feel fulfilled at last.

Clara still occupied herself by examining dog poo and crawling under tables, but the magnificence around us was so vivid and continuous that it hardly mattered. Whatever she did, my daughter, I still had my feast. I could sit with her all morning in the traffic-free Piazza Navona and bask in the beauty of Bernini's fountains while she pried ancient horse manure from the cobblestones.

I could eat the most voluptuous ravioli in walnut sauce while she poured salt into her water glass, and I could watch gorgeous Romans saunter past while she rubbed peach-almond ice cream into her hair.

So this was my lesson, which I'll pack with me next time: Surround your small child with exotic environs, and in between the spills and breaks and vanishing acts, you need only lift up your gaze to reap your reward.

SOME THOUGHTS ON
GRABBING WISDOM TO GO

Brushes with Royalty

Clara wouldn't speak to me all day last Thursday because I was going to see the Queen and she was not. She was purse-mouthed and cross-armed. She kept fixing me with a stony glare, as if I were deliberately barring my five-year-old dearest from a rare and wondrous vision.

Of course, children were not invited to Queen Elizabeth II's jubilee gala at Toronto's Roy Thomson Hall, but I also felt I was protecting my daughter from the inevitable devastation she would feel upon realizing that the Queen bore no resemblance to a Barbie in a cone hat. After a steady diet of snow queens and wicked queens and princess-and-the pea queens, my daughter would be shocked by the real Queen, with her steel-grey sausage curls and sensible coats.

Still, there is an appealing thread of narrative continuity between her fairy tales and real life in the mere *fact* that there is, actually, a queen. This keeps open the possibility of there being flower fairies as well, and possibly even mermaids and elves, although ideally not monsters. So Mummy was dressing up to see *the Queen*, and that was sufficiently exciting for Clara to eventually surmount her huff. I, on the other hand, was feeling faintly disturbed by the fact that I was going to see the Queen. My mother, who is a Canadian senator, had invited me to this jubilee gala as her date. The occasion, my mother advised, was black tie and long dress, which is to say the fanciest party clothes I've ever been asked to don, ever, ever. Including to my own wedding.

Yet it wasn't a party. It was a concert. It was the modern equivalent of Henry VIII clapping his hands at court and shouting "bring on the minstrels." We were all meant to gather together in the most sumptuous clothes we could find in order to sit in a darkened theatre watching—as it turned out—the rock band the Tragically Hip. A very fine-clothed lady sitting ahead of me in row G hunched over and stuck her fingers in her ears as the Hip played, her silken blouse quivering on her shoulders as she tensed with displeasure. I found that rude. Would the Queen do such a thing? Certainly not.

In any event, with the evening still ahead of me, I went to Shoppers Drug Mart and bought some nail polish. I haven't polished my short uneven mommy nails in years, but it seemed necessary. The Queen would expect dainty nails. Not that I was going to meet her. There was no receiving line. Getting fancy for my wedding was a no-brainer, but this occasion felt more . . . *je ne sais quoi . . . qui va voir* my nails anyway? Who would be there to admire my finery? If it was just a question of keeping pace with the Queen, then I wasn't sure that a sleeveless brocade dress with threads of gold and lavender and a shimmering silk overcoat were appropriate. A sparkly tent-dress was more in line.

Oh dear. Well, I hauled out my Yves Saint Laurent wedding shoes and figured no one would notice that my daughter had drawn on the heels with green marker. Then I donned my outfit and a gorgeous pair of gold earrings lent to me by my mother and snaked slowly along the walls of the house trying to avoid Geoffrey as I headed for the door. Unscathed by cracker spittle, we toddled off in our stilettos, my mother and I, leaving my daughter enormously impressed and jealous, as if she were Cinderella and we were the stepsisters. "Ta ta! We're off to the ball!"

We arrived at six-forty-five and discovered that we had an hour and a half to kill until we could sit down, with nothing on offer but soda water and fleeting shreds of chicken satay whisked past us before we could reach out. So we milled about hungrily, now and then bumping into Mum's friends. Nobody seemed to notice that I'd polished my nails.

The invitation list had been drawn up by the prime minister and consisted primarily of people over fifty with Liberal Party connections. I saw former Ontario premier David Peterson, for instance, who has become the political equivalent of celebrities on the D list who are game to do *Hollywood Squares*, which is to say that you can count on him to pop up at galas. When we finally got to sit down in the auditorium, all the politicians began jumping up in their seats and waving at one another and cracking excited jokes like school chums on a field trip.

At quarter after eight, the Toronto Symphony suddenly started up a fanfare, and all necks craned leftward and upward for the arrival of the Queen. *Da da da daaah da da da da da dum dum.* It was kind of thrilling. One felt fleetingly swept up in a current of genuine power. This was not the Queen sweeping into a ballroom, mind you, but a Queen creeping sideways into her seat in a theatre, excuse me, excuse me, with one hand holding up the hem of her sparkly tent-dress. She was preceded by a small group of elderly ladies sporting pearl chokers and puffed blouses.

"Who are they?" I asked my mother.

"Those are her ladies-in-waiting."

"No way!" All of a sudden I had this epiphany, like whoa! She's a real queen! Like those other queens from days of yore! Where are their cone hats?

"What on earth do they do?" I whispered to Mum. "Do they help her put on her bra?"

"I suppose they accompany her," my mother guessed vaguely, "and probably act as her confidantes about what have you." The Queen is no longer permitted to chop off their heads, so relations are doubtless convivial.

"Maybe they have an investment club," a friend of mine speculated later. "Or play Chinese bridge." Perhaps they go back to the Queen's chambers after each minstrel show and succumb to the giggles. I could imagine them musing about the woman in the gala who belted out "MacArthur Park" with so much reverb on her mike that you couldn't hear any of the lyrics except for the preposterous chorus: "Someone left the cake out in the rain! I'll never find the recipe again!" This, with full symphonic accompaniment. A lament for you, Your Majesty, concerning wet cake, on the occasion of your golden jubilee.

My overall sense of the occasion was crystallized in the videotaped tributes offered between live acts. Canadians commented on the Queen's fifty years of ribbon cutting and waving. Good for you, for . . . uh . . . well, you didn't defeat the Spanish Armada or found the Church of England, but . . . darn it, good for you for being the Queen! You *wave*, girl! Susan Aglukark pointed out that the Queen had shared the same period of history as her own Inuit community, which is an observation of such indirect import that you could say it to a pigeon.

But that's all right. We may not know what she's for, but we do love Her Majesty, and she loves us back. She even went onstage and shook hands with Canada's most beloved rock band. That is grace most becoming of a queen.

And What News of the King?

A few days after the gala, my friend Pier and I went to see a movie, and then decided to have a drink before heading home at midnight to our small sleeping children. The nearest bar was in Toronto's Four Seasons Hotel, in swankest Yorkville, the home-away-from-home for all the Hollywood folk who drift through town these days to make their movies on the cheap or to promote them at the festival.

Neither Pier nor I had ever been to this overpriced out-of-towner bar before, but we walked in, worrying faintly about the fact that we were wearing jeans and juice-stained mommy T-shirts and might even be requested to leave. The sleek brass-and-mahogany bar was jammed with well-heeled customers smoking and yapping, so we felt lucky when we spied a just-vacated corner spot, tip and empty glasses still upon the table. We sat down and began pondering what to drink when the waitress came over and smilingly explained that there was actually a line-up for the tables and that the "two gentlemen at the bar over there have been waiting for this one."

Ah, *c'est la vie.* We weren't surprised or offended. We got up and headed for the bar ourselves, figuring we could order drinks and just sort of stand about. En route, we bumped into the two middle-aged men who had dibs on the table, one of whom grabbed my elbow and started gushing about how grateful he was that we'd been kind enough to surrender our seats.

"I have terrible back pain," he explained, blowing booze breath in my face.

He was a faded, rumpled fellow with too-small eyes and a receding hairline, and I was thinking that it was a bit odd for him to be so profusely thankful when we'd so obviously jumped the queue. It's not like we'd volunteered to climb out of an ambulance for him, limping off with fractured tibias. But then, all of a sudden, it dawned on me that this man was the actor Liam Neeson, whom I had last seen towering elegantly over the throngs in the movie *Schindler's List.*

Instantly my knees began to shake. I went from being puzzled and uninterested to feeling *physically handicapped* in one fell click of my brain. His celebrity, and nothing more, just the fact of it, had the power to alter my physiological state. How strange is that? I ask you. Now I needed the table back, and he had only himself to blame. Of course, being a WASP lady, I refused to even admit that I'd recognized him, instead simply grinned and uttered some reply—which, because I was trembling, came across as unintelligible, as if I were muttering at him in Yiddish. Then I accepted his offer to buy me and Pier a glass of wine and proceeded—after he'd settled himself down at "our" table, while we stood at the bar—to pick the most expensive Chardonnay on the menu.

Pier and I speculated that Neeson had been so thankful to us because he wrongly assumed that we had given up our table to personally accommodate him, Liam Neeson. One reaches a certain level of fame and ceases believing that people observe decorum for its own sake rather than because they want to be sycophantic expressly to you.

I was thinking about this strange, unanchored power of celebrity—how an otherwise unremarkable person can make your knees shake when you find out his name—when I attended the IdeaCity conference in downtown Toronto.

The buzz among attendees at this conference was that the big names, like Peter Jennings, wouldn't be the interesting speakers. If you wanted ideas, you had to perk up your ears at the mousy scholars and shy inventors who walked onstage. So what was the function of the big names? When Jennings took the stage, he actually confided: "I haven't got the vaguest bloody idea why I'm here." I suppose it was simply to excite everyone with his presence. To eat muffins at a conference with Peter Jennings, why, is that not the *ne plus ultra*?

With all due respect to the man, this is what's so vexing to me about our present culture. We live in a culture of celebrity, where famous people can make us tremble, yet they offer no substance—no ideas, no leadership, no inspirational models of virtue. They are, after all, mostly entertainers by trade; it was never their mission to reincarnate royalty. I'm sure this is why actors are always yammering on in interviews about how they actually have drug addictions and dysfunctional families and eating disorders. It is as if they are trying to deflect our hopeless reverence by pointing out that they're not heroes and revolutionaries and geniuses—they're just *actors* for chrissake.

As Sue Erikson Bloland observed in an essay about fame in the *Atlantic Monthly*, people who achieve celebrity are often characterized by monstrous insecurity and self-loathing, these being the very qualities that propel them to grasp for approval. For us to take this neurotic drive of theirs and turn it into something worthy of worship is essentially ridiculous, is it not? All we wind up worshiping is the panicked pursuit of self-aggrandizement itself. There are exceptions, notable among them the Irish rock star Bono. His amazing efforts to become a gadfly to first world governments for third world causes reveal the rare alchemy of star dust and altruism. Bono showed up in Canada shortly before the federal election in 2004 to nag Prime Minister Paul Martin about increasing the foreign aid budget. Martin agreed, which promptly inspired an opposition candidate to complain. "I think that's just the prime minister trying to get some star power around himself," Stephen Harper told the press. "We all know what that game is."

But Bono had a succinct reply. "Yes, I'm being used," he said cheerfully. "I want to be used. That's my job here, to provide applause when someone does the right and courageous thing and to provide criticism when they don't."

One of my favourite speakers at IdeaCity was the Montreal crime journalist Michel Auger, who became famous for being shot, in the parking lot of *Le Journal de Montréal*, presumably by the organized criminals he'd been writing about. Ever since, he has won numerous national awards and invitations to conferences, and even an offer for a lucrative contract to promote Viagra. "This conference is supposed to be a meeting of minds," he wryly observed, "but I'm here for my body." With wonderful candour and humility, Auger was pointing out that the fame of the incident itself had conferred upon him greater import as a thinker.

"I was a regular reporter," he explained. "And then, the day I was shot, I became a great reporter." *Figurez-vous*. With leadership and leading ideas framed this way, is it any wonder that truth is up for grabs and that its purveyors are increasingly mercantile?

To Get Famous in America, You Must Set Your Alarm

Going on a book tour is an interesting way to measure what it takes to be influential in the modern world. I remember the shocked revelation I had with my first book, when I learned that—well, I learned two things really— that it was a very bad idea to publish a book shortly after Princess Diana died in a car accident and that, further- more, being influential in the world has very little to do with what you have written down on paper and a great deal to do with how coherent you are on early morning TV shows.

I learned this because I once had the grand, amazing opportunity to be on *Good Morning America*. It *was* grand and amazing: They flew me down to New York; they put me up in a hotel; they arranged for a limo to collect me in the morning. The only trouble was that, being a new mother, I was equally captivated by the possibility of watching movies on the hotel TV without anyone bugging me. I could watch any old movie I liked! It didn't have to be the forty-fifth showing of *Balto* or a grainy BBC

production of *Frog and Toad*. It could be something adult,
and I could lie there like a barnyard pig flicking at flies
with my ears rather than having those same ears tuned,
tensed as a hunted fox, to the cries of a child down the
hall. I ordered room service and had a major mud wallow.
Indeed, I so revelled in this opportunity that I watched two
whole movies. Two! And then, I slept through my alarm.

If you wanted to recreate the conditions that child-
care experts recommend for babies with colic, you would
put them in a hotel room with no sound but the white
noise of the air conditioner. Then, block out light with
heavy draperies. Ensure an utter cryptlike stillness. Be
certain that they stayed up the night before until two A.M.
sobbing as they watched *The English Patient*. And *voilà*.
Cranky babies and mothers on book tour, sleeping like
logs.

I finally—and abruptly—awoke to the impatient rapping
of the limo driver on my door and, after glancing at the
clock, shot to a standing position with enough fuck-fuck-
fuck adrenaline to catapult a cow to Pluto. *Fuhhhhhk*. I
hopped around the room, trying to haul on my nylons.
Within seconds I had pulled on my clothes and flung open
the door, still fumbling with the straps of my shoes. The
irritated limo driver advised me without sympathy that I
had ten minutes, exactly, until airtime.

In retrospect, words cannot sufficiently commend the
makeup and hair crew of *Good Morning America*, who
managed to process me from sound asleep to made-
over-with-helmet-hair in under five minutes. It was

remarkable—it truly was. If they could have speed-spritzed my brain so that I wasn't seated there on *GMA*'s happy set as alert as bread dough, for all the consumers of pancakes in America's entire chain of Denny's to see, that would have helped too.

"So, Patricia," began the host, as I stared into the middle distance and thought the thoughts of somebody reading the ingredients on a cereal box, "you have stated in your controversial new book that blahdeeblah, hoo hoo hoo, and we have a critic on satellite hookup from Texas who has been up since yesterday and is frothing at the bit like Gloria Allred on crack to oppose you. Can you defend yourself, please?"

". . . Uh . . ."

"Well," the host swiftly added, "you clearly believe this controversial and complicated argument, as you laid out in your book, and what is it? We need you to summarize it in a sound bite right this instant before we cut to your critic."

"Um . . ."

Ah, so, you see? This is the quandary. The first step to being influential in America is to wake up on time. If half of the country is religious and derives its wisdom from the Bible or the Talmud or the Quran, the other half derives it from people who are peppy.

One morning, years later but also very early, I found myself in the studio of a local Vancouver television show, waiting my turn to sit on a bar stool and chat with the two preternaturally jocular hosts. Ahead of me in the lineup was a broad-chested man with a brush cut and a pointy nose, somewhat reminiscent of a badger, who was promoting his book, *Law of Attraction: The Science of Attracting More of What You Want and Less of What You Don't!* His name was Michael J. Losier, and his big-shouldered physicality put me in mind of the homicide cops in their ill-fitting brown suits and shiny black shoes that I used to interview in Long Island when I was on a crime beat.

Losier, I learned, listening to the interview, was a former provincial bureaucrat with the British Columbia Ministry of Transportation, who had somehow discovered that he knew the universal law of attraction and could parlay his wisdom into a career on the book-and-lecture circuit. He was very excited, you could tell. Indeed, his excitement and good mood had evidently assisted him with his book, through some sort of process involving vibes. "Vibes," he explained to the TV hosts, "are really vibrations, which are moods." I wrote this down in my notebook. Someone handed me a mug of coffee. Then I caught Losier saying, "So, the law of attraction checks in to see which mood you're in. I've attracted twenty-one people to help me with this book."

He then summarized the steps involved in learning to live your life according to the law of attraction, and I no longer remember any of them except for the last one, which I jotted down. "Allow it," he advised the hosts, "that's the last step." I couldn't understand what that meant for the longest time, but then I finally realized that it meant: "believe."

There was a commercial break. Michael Losier left, and I took the stool that had just been warmed by his vibes. The law of attraction checked its watch, and I said, "Uh . . ."

Speak to Your Dog and Grow Rich

If you are a peppy sort of person who is wondering how to make money, I highly recommend the Learning Annex as a possible venue for employment. I came to this conclusion after noticing that the Learning Annex itself offered a course—by someone named Dottie Walters—called "Speak and Grow Rich." In her picture, Dottie Walters sports a lovely leopard print hat, and she teaches people like you and me how to turn—just stuff we know—into a lucrative speaking and growing-rich career.

I found out about Dottie Walters shortly after I had completed my book tour, to no financial avail, and had just noticed that Michael Losier was teaching seminars at the Learning Annex on the law of attraction. I figured maybe Dottie Walters was onto something. This got me wondering who else was on their roster, and that—to make a long story short—is how I wound up spending two hours in the company of Rochelle Gai Rodney, area pet telepathist, who explained the trick to overcoming all known laws of nature in order to read pets' minds.

Of course, a cynic would wish to know, who were the

chumps surrendering cash for such ridiculous hocus pocus? Well, I was, for one. I'll do anything to overcome my current domestic impasse, in which I never have even the remotest clue what my dog wants, and he never has the slightest, faintest inkling what I'm saying to him.

Kevin, who is my dog, is a cross between border collie and Basenji, which means that half of him descends from one of the smartest breeds known and the other half from, easily, the stupidest. He is highly alert, and unable to grasp a single thing. Kevin's entire communicative repertoire, whether he wants water, food, company, exercise, permission to jump on the sofa, relief from boredom, some painkillers, a toy, or a conversation about the hydro bill, consists of padding up to me and staring. He does this about fifty times a day, just stares brightly without moving a muscle, and after seven years of living together, I still don't know what he wants. We coexist in a state of profound mutual incomprehension.

Sometimes I think it doesn't matter that I don't know what he wants, because we have nothing in common. Whatever he wants will be something that I don't want. He probably wants me to get up from my desk and go outside for the rest of the day to barrel after squirrels. I don't want to.

If I were my husband, I'd just let Kevin stare at me until his eyeballs fell out and not worry about it. He takes Kevin for his walks, ensures that his kibble is replenished, keeps the bathroom door ajar so that Kevin can drink from the toilet, and lets him sleep on the bed. That's it. Done.

But I'm a woman, and a mother, and I worry about how everyone is feeling. So I paid the Learning Annex their fee and took my chair in a classroom on a cold night, flipped open my notebook, and prepared to read Kevin's mind.

Rochelle Gai Rodney is a former government bureaucrat who suddenly had the revelation that she wasn't meant to push pencils because she knew what pets are thinking. Rodney arrived for her class carrying a Siamese cat named Moose, whom she introduced as her teaching assistant. Rodney put him down and Moose shot into the closet, where he remained for the next two hours.

"By the end of this class, you will be hearing Moose communicate telepathically," Rodney assured us, beaming. "She's just going to be invisible for a while. That will help you get used to communicating with pets at a distance."

The twenty or so women in the classroom nodded avidly. We perked up our senses and eagerly awaited a message from Moose, such as "Get me the hell out of here." In the meantime, Rodney, a small, happy woman with a disarming giggle, explained what she knew about animal communication.

"The thing that animals want most in their life is to be heard," she said, sitting on a desk and swinging her legs to and fro, "especially the birds. They really have a lot to say because they travel around the world." That's true, isn't it? But they're birds. Surely they aren't going to wing their way back from Florida hoping to discuss the election? "You'll be amazed at what animals have to say," Rodney insisted. "They may want to design your cottage. I've had a consult with a pug who was an English banker in its previous life."

Oh God. What if Kevin wants to design my cottage? Forget it—he'd create a giant squirrel baffle with fifteen toilets.

"Don't analyze; don't edit," Rodney warned us, about receiving messages in our minds. "Just be willing to say 'That was real.' I'm at the point where I've convinced myself that I'm totally accurate. So, just believe in yourself. It's real. I'm getting paid to do it, so it must be." I'm just not going to touch that logic.

Rodney had the class divide into pairs in order to practise telepathic communication. The woman beside me was to tune into Kevin, and I was to pick up the thoughts of her cat. We both looked horrified, which suggested that we shared a certain insecurity about the task at hand. But what could we do? We'd paid our money, and here we were, so I offered that her cat was under the bed and wanted to go out. She countered that Kevin was lying in front of the fireplace and also wanted to go out.

We reported our findings to the class, feeling like a pair of Pinocchios. On the way home, I daydreamed of ways to earn money by teaching at the Learning Annex: how to breed hens that lay golden eggs, for instance, or a seminar on how to wave your hands up and down and wish upon stars. My husband suggested that I contact Rodney for a personal consultation with Kevin.

"Let her go *mano a mano* with Kevin," he urged. "Just

her and him." I hesitated for weeks because Rodney charges $160 an hour for a private session. That's a lot of coin. That's like a lawyer's fee. In the end, however, while filming a television segment on kids and pets, I introduced the telepathist to her subject, who was conked out on the dining room floor making snuffling sounds, and asked her what he thought.

"He says that you, as a family, should lighten up and enjoy yourselves more," Rodney reported. Otherwise, she said, Kevin is happy with his lot in life, which is to be a teacher to us, to help us connect with our energies, and to receive messages from him. Oh God, this is just a vicious circle. *What* messages?

My husband interrupted with his own inquiry: "Ask Kevin who killed my nephew's pet gerbil, him or Biscuit?" (Biscuit is my sister's psycho-frisky golden retriever, who can't be in a room two seconds without knocking something over with her tail. She also drags socks out of the laundry hamper to chew on, is the neighbourhood's principal consumer of poo, and generally drives my sister bananas.)

Rodney asked the deeply asleep Kevin if he was responsible for a certain gerbil's corpse appearing beneath my nephew's bed last Memorial Day weekend. Then she looked at me. "Kevin says it was sad, it happened very fast, but his back was turned at the time." Upon hearing this, my husband had to leave the room and bray with laughter in the yard. Meanwhile, Rodney offered to tune into Biscuit long-distance in Montreal, to determine if Kevin was evading responsibility here. A moment later, she announced that yes, it was Biscuit. Biscuit had killed the gerbil, "and she's not sorry."

I thanked the pet telepathist and ran like a bat out of hell to call my sister with the news. "BISCUIT DID IT—AND SHE'S NOT SORRY!" My sister laughed so hard she fell off her office chair. That's gotta be worth 160 bucks, don't you think?

Ode to Doreen Virtue, Ph.D.

What I respect most about Doreen Virtue, Ph.D., a serene and comely counselling psychologist from Nashville who teaches widely across North America, is that she is the only living human being, as far as I am aware, who has co-authored a book with the angelic realm. This ought to be world historic news, and I don't know why it isn't. But her paperback, *Angel Therapy: Healing Messages for Every Area of Your Life* by Doreen Virtue, Ph.D. and the Angelic Realm, is a startling authorial collaboration. According to Doreen Virtue, who presents seminars at the Learning Annex, among other places, the angelic realm dictates messages to her on everything from "job search" to "break-ups." They even provide a blurb on the back of the book.

As such, this is an extraordinary development in the annals of modern theological dispute. Even as scholars and clerics debate in endless papers the number, purpose, meaning, and veracity of the heavenly host, here is the entire angelic realm—HELLO?—present and accounted for through the mind of Doreen Virtue, just waiting for the faculty at Union Theological Seminary in New York to stand up and take notice. I like to think that the pope is aware of the angelic realm communicating through Doreen Virtue or at least that another high Christian official is, perhaps the Archbishop of Canterbury. But it is depressingly common, these days, for fantastic revelations to remain within their own strict disciplines of academe, where sociologists are unaware of the data compiled by criminologists and so forth, so perhaps the same blinkered mindset holds true for Christianity.

I am moved by what the angelic realm says to me about food.

"Earth speaks to you through her offspring, the living plants that you eat," the angelic realm writes. "Think of it this way: your dinner meal is a meeting in which messages and ideas are exchanged." I had certainly never thought of it that way before, so now I am in a better position to know that escarole talks to me as I chew it. To be honest, I can't discern the spiritual import of that, but I realize that I cannot presume.

The angelic realm is very good on dating. "Your essence is charming," they write, "and you needn't worry that you would lapse into a being that bores or repels others." That is such sweet advice. They then promise to be there for you to check in with as you hunker down at the Olive Garden or the Rainbow Room or wherever you go, but they add diplomatically: "Granted, we may come along on your date, but you can also block us out at any time you choose." Thank God, right? Awkward, impulsive, heated sex without being observed by the entire angelic realm, please.

I know that Doreen Virtue has trained many, many other Americans to be certified angel therapy counsellors, bringing the gracious and gentle advice of the angelic realm to humans, for a moderate fee. I wanted to ask her about this and started hoping that she would show up on *Larry King Live*, where I could call in for free. Not many people watch as much CNN as I do, given that I have had it on constantly ever since 9/11 just in case I miss something, but certainly some people will have noticed, as I have, that Larry King has a fondness for interviewing people who pluck answers out of thin air.

This does not bother me, for I understand that these people are tuning in to a frequency I cannot detect. For that matter, my TV tunes into a frequency I can neither detect, exactly, nor explain to my children with confidence. As far as my household is concerned, Larry King himself is as much a leap of faith as the talkative deceased relatives of his viewers.

One Good Friday, not long ago, I went down to the Metro Convention Centre, where faith ran its consoling current through the downstairs exhibit hall.

"Oh, look at this," a palm reader murmured, tracing lines on my hand with her pen. "You can communicate with aliens." Her announcement was certain and full of admiration. She sat back in her chair. We were in a corner booth at the Psychic and Astrology Expo, where God had been trumped by "personalized healthy balls."

The palm reader, seeking confirmation, gazed into my face with baleful blue eyes that wavered in and out of focus behind smudged bifocals. I knew of my powers all along, did I not?

"Oh, you're psychic, girl." She squeezed my hand. She nodded. I nodded back. My face must have been utterly blank. I usually say, "I know what you mean" and contribute some confession to encourage a fledgling connection. But I've never dated an alien, haven't written them any letters. I'm not going to bother searching my mind. She nodded again, more briefly—"it's true, girl"— and moved on to warnings from the left side of my palm about impending osteoporosis.

Flipping my hand back and forth like a disembodied object, patting it, drawing on it, she added that I would make lots of money after I'm forty. I had a "karmic crisis" when I was fourteen, she noted, possibly referring to the night I necked with Chris Sutherland in Garth Somebody's basement and got labelled a slut at school.

And I make someone else do the dishes, "Right?" Nudge, nudge, the sharing of a conspiratorial chuckle.

"Oh! Here's something really good!" She clapped. "You're never gonna have a nervous breakdown, lady!" Well, the definition slides.

In truth, it doesn't matter what she said. Psychic fairs are like red-light districts for the heart. Lonely people cruise their aisles, looking for a stranger they can pay to understand them, someone to say "it'll be all right," the way a lover would. I paid my palm reader thirty-five dollars to make me feel important, and loved, and revealed. "Yes, I can tell what kind of person you are," a handwriting analyst informed an overweight young man with carroty hair, one of several solitary young men in the hall. And she'll only fathom the good things. Never that he's a jerk, or a man about to die.

"People take what they need," an off-duty psychic observed to another in the cafeteria upstairs, both of them drawing on cigarettes, tired from guessing secrets all day. Their potential clients wandered quietly and carefully through the aisles, sizing up the Renowned British Psychic, the Famous Irish Psychic, the International Psychic, the Aura Photo booth, and Yogi Narayana, Super Psychic, who once predicted that Margaret Trudeau would become an evangelist. All the seers had snared a client. There must have been eighty lives being sensed all at once here, in a clamorous traffic jam of auras and vibrations. It's curious that the psychics don't get addled when they work these fairs. They must pick up random frequencies, like crossed conversations on a cellphone, from one another's clients just a few feet away. Maria Graciette of Hollywood presided over her Tarot in a leopard-print blouse, facing a woman in a fuchsia pantsuit. Was she "feeling" that this woman wanted her mum to buy her a horse? Because across the aisle, the gemstone reader Marlene had an adolescent client, shy, with braces. I had seen two of the psychics before on this circuit. I blew one hundred dollars between them one awful November day about five years ago when I couldn't stand the friendless silence of my flat. Marie-Claire was a beautiful French medium from Montreal with a seductively husky voice.

"There is a man," she told me then. "He is an older man, who is ill. But he will get better!"

It was happy news, except that I didn't know any older men who were ill. I was the one who felt ill with my longing. She watched me pensively, knowing she'd gotten it wrong. The other one I saw was now a few booths down the aisle, with the same display of newspaper clips he had had before, showing that he helped the police find drowned children and stolen jewels. I remember he seduced me with admiring comments about how old my soul was. Then he told me I was allergic to cheese.

I wonder what else I could learn, if I had four thousand dollars to burn and every seer in the hall got their chance to see right through me. My fortunes would be infinite, my talents manifold, my food aversions legion. I doubt anyone would cough up a forwarding address for the aliens. But there's always hope. That's a prediction the psychics need to bank on.

You Don't Want to Know What Your Therapist Is Thinking

I was complaining to a friend the other day that I would sooner crawl through a sewer than fly on a plane, to which she replied, "How irrational," and I said, "Yes, I *know* that, but so is your phobia of cotton batting." Whereupon we agreed that our fears might merit a little bit of therapy.

So my friend said: I don't know anyone good. Why not shop around?

Excellent idea, I thought, because I'd been hearing about this trend of online therapy. Enterprising psychotherapists the world over have been throwing up websites to advertise their skill at plumbing the depths of your soul. All you have to do is submit credit card information and you can get counselling via live chat, video conferencing, or email without ever leaving your home.

This is actually perfect, because I hate the traditional process of acquiring a therapist. You have to ask around, which gets people gossiping, and in exchange they hand over some name on a piece of paper with an extremely vague testimonial, like: "He's really nice" or "I found him to be quite nice" or "She didn't say one single thing in six months, just stared at me, but she was nice."

Nice, schmice, what *school* are they from? Freudian, Jungian, Gestaltian, past-lives, or dolphin-assisted? You have to know where these therapists are getting their theories about you because there isn't one grand therapist perspective on the universe. Some of them are convinced that you were abused as a child; others think you're governed by electric currents in your brain. I know all about this because I have been dogged by ridiculous episodes of anxiety throughout my adult life, and this has flung me onto various mysterious shores. I have collapsed upon the proverbial couches, gasping and sputtering and evincing a terror of getting cancer from barbecued meat or being creamed by an SUV, and at various times I have been told that it is my mother's fault, that patriarchy and internalized anger are to blame, that it's a chemical imbalance, or a repressed memory of being sacrificed to Satan.

The advantage to cybertherapy is that the therapists trumpet their perspective on their websites. Thus we have, for example, "Reality Therapy On-line Services" based on "choice theory" as taught at the William Glasser Institute in California. "The goal of reality therapy," states the institute's website, "is to help people re-connect." How that works, specifically, is all written out right there for you to scroll through until your head hurts.

If reconnecting isn't for you, try an email exchange with Dr. Robert F. Sarmiento of Houston, Texas, whose website advocates SMART therapy, which is Self-Management and Recovery Training, "based on Rational-Emotive Behaviour Therapy."

Alternatively, you can pour your heart out to Alec Gore, a Neuro-Linguistic Programmer who offers "The Road" approach, which distinguishes itself from other therapies, his website argues, by being "solution-oriented." Indeed, the boast on Gore's site is that: "You have reached one of the most innovative and effective services in accelerated human change." You have also reached a man who is actually practising psychotherapy in Hong Kong, and that is one of the most intriguing aspects of online counselling. Patients are no longer confined to therapists within physical reach, which is a tremendous advantage to people outside of major cities and also to people who feel culturally and linguistically displaced. A recent immigrant to the United States, for instance, could perhaps find counselling from her home country on the Net. Write home to France: "*J'ai beaucoup d'ennui.*" (Translation: "I am le tired.")

Of course, the disadvantage to this cross-border fluidity is the truly stunning, frontier-style lack of regulation. With therapists available from so many different states and nations, well, Buyer Beware.

The first time I launched myself into this world of anonymous therapists I surfed aimlessly, and eventually decided to submit my neurosis at random to three different therapists. I prattle-typed to each about my phobia of not smoking and, come to think of it, my phobia of the dentist and of flying, and how I lapsed into this sort of obstinate paralysis when it came to self-improvement of any kind, really, and was also horrified of diets and Pilates and climate change and. . . .

It eventually occurred to me that successful patients in the world of cyberpsychology really have to know how to type. Ambrose, for instance, types like a chicken pecking for seeds, bent over his keyboard with two cocked fingers and a focused gleam in his eye. He pulls off a sentence in the time it takes me to speed-type the entire plot of a dream I've just had about Gwyneth Paltrow and her baby, Apple, and how for some reason I moved in with them, and then I pulled a one-hundred-year-old hair out of my mouth that belonged to an ancient mariner. And what if a prospective patient had writer's block? What if the very act of writing made them feel inadequate and consequently more depressed?

In any event, a couple of days after I sent the email about smoking, I received the following message: "Be a non-smoker in 7 days!!! With Kick-It. Guaranteed." Oh, that perky spam. If you think hucksters aren't monitoring psychotherapy exchanges along with everything else, you can now put that delusion to rest.

Next, from Adriane St. Clare, a psychologist in Fortuna, California, I received this message in reply to my cry for help: "Your problem of paralysis and inability to stop smoking may be related to the anisorder you suffered from earlier in your life." Hmmm. Interesting. Anisorder? What is that? A typo? He concluded: "I would highly recommend a face-to-face treatment, such as EMDR, to assure the most effective results." Oh, EMDR. Right. And that would be what?

To decipher babble, please provide credit card info here.

Some weeks later Dr. Rob Sarmiento of Houston, to whom I shelled out forty U.S. dollars, sent me a kind email suggesting that I do the "reality check" quiz on his site and otherwise try to engage in cognitive-behavioural therapy. "You might also want to observe what urge-causing thoughts you have when you feel like smoking, such as 'I need a cigarette' or 'I can't quit.'"

Amazing! Those really are the urge-causing thoughts that I have!

"Once you have identified the thoughts," Sarmiento continued, "you can start questioning them, for example, 'How uncomfortable will it be on a one-to-ten scale, with ten being boiled in oil?'"

That's hard. I don't know. I've never been boiled in oil. Nor have I ever had my head sawed off with a butter knife, which I suspect would also hurt worse than quitting smoking, but I just don't see them as competing options.

Not to knock Dr. Sarmiento, because he then sent me an envelope full of fridge magnets with reality check lists on them, and a wallet card proclaiming itself an Official Human Being Licence.

Let me tell you: I may have been a smoker, but I'm no rodent, or a plant either, and I have the papers to prove it.

The Five-Minute Phobia Cure

Leafing through *Psychology Today* in the allergist's office the other day, I came across an ad for a Five-Minute Phobia Cure. Apparently, a Dr. Roger Callahan of Indian Wells, California, has pioneered a new psychological technique called Thought Field Therapy, whereby phobias and other traumas can be fixed with a few light karate chops to your collarbone and forehead.

Phobias, Callahan has explained on such early morning shows as *Good Morning America,* are perturbances in the "energy field" of a thought. You must physically remove the perturbances in order to get on with the business of riding in elevators without screaming or staying calm in the presence of spiders.

Well, I'm tired of getting absolutely hysterical on airplanes. So I procured a video copy of the *Five-Minute Phobia Cure* for forty dollars and gave it a try. Callahan, who looks disconcertingly like Burt Reynolds, demonstrates his theory by plucking paper clips from an elastic band. One thought field perturbance down, four to go. *Pluck, pluck.* He must be on to something. Never mind the complex inner labyrinth of neuroses so revered by psychoanalysts. People want their problems fixed, and they want them fixed NOW. Okay?

Okay. The therapy sequence in the video involves a guy in a red T-shirt, who must be Callahan's apprentice, posed like an aerobics instructor at the front of a class and taking you through the following paces. First he gets you to summon a mental picture of your phobia, which "brings up the thought field." In my case, the image of strangely elated Arab men taking control of my airplane, which was supposed to be flying from Toronto to Cancún but instead is being steered into Mount Rushmore, comes obediently into view. Then you must do this:

Tap four or five times under your eye, then under your arm, then on your collarbone, then your hand. Waggle your eyes, hum a tune, and count to five.

Voilà.

I wanted to test this cure, but since my plane phobia would entail driving to the airport and plunging off a roof, I enlisted Ambrose instead.

"Can you just come down here for a second and try this phobia cure?" I asked.

"Go away," he responded, sensing trouble. "I'm reading."

"Please, just for five minutes! I want to see if it cures your horror of mayonnaise."

"No."

My husband is what Callahan calls a "skeptical stranger." Skeptics are perfect for demonstrating the efficacy of thought field therapy, Callahan claims, because they're not suggestible. Bribed with the promise that I'd vacuum the car, Ambrose finally agreed to watch the video. He tapped under his eye, on his arm, and at his collarbone, sighing loudly. He waggled his eyes.

I whipped out a jar of Hellmann's. "*Arrrrgggghhhhhhhh!*" he shouted.

On the video, the words "psychological reversal" flashed on the screen. Callahan believes that some people are subject to psychological blocks, or reversals, that make them impervious to his treatment. Thus, he has devised a thirty-second treatment for your treatment block.

"Tap on your hand and say three times: I accept myself even though I have these problems."

Ambrose went along, glaring at me, then repeated the phobia cure of tapping, humming, and counting.

"So, now what do you think?" I asked, approaching tentatively with my jar.

"GET AWAY FROM ME WITH THAT MAYONNAISE!"

Maybe we did it wrong. Callahan has tapped on people on all the major American network talk shows, to great effect.

If you reject the theory that phobias are random electromagnetic perturbations in the brain, you have many other theories to choose from: early childhood trauma, instinct, atavism, and generalized anxiety, to name a few. According to William I. Miller, author of a fascinating book called *The Anatomy of Disgust*, many phobias are really a conflation of fear and disgust, relating to our need for an ordered universe. We are horrified by disorder and chaos, such as weeds growing pellmell in a garden, overly lush vegetation, or the body turned inside out—oozing, slimy viscera, what Miller calls "thick, greasy life." So, people have phobias of eggs, vomit, honey, and other slippery substances, which are really an anxiety about the corruptible boundaries of the body.

Interesting. Unlike pure fear, which invites a fight-or-flight response, the nature of the horrifying is the apprehension that there is no escape. To fight the dandelion or sunny-side-up egg would involve touching it, which evokes terror of contamination. To flee it would mean that it wasn't all around you, and even *in* you, which in itself is the essence of what's horrifying. Mad cow disease. Avian flu. SARS. "The disgusting can possess us," Miller writes, and "fill us with creepy, almost eerie feelings of not being quite in control, of being haunted."

We fear being overrun, and we also fear falling apart. Try this. Nothing is quite so disgusting in the mouth as a single hair, as proved in an experiment Miller cites in which a group of toddlers under observation, quite possibly including my own, happily ate dog feces, grasshoppers, and a whole small dried fish but completely freaked out about hair being in their mouths or on their tongues.

We are also horrified by the uncanny: "the unsettlingness of the effigy," explains Miller. Clowns, for instance. They confuse our perceptions of real and unreal. Particularly, I would say, when the clowns turn out to be serial killers, as in the news about John Wayne Gacy of Chicago, who made a point of (a) entertaining children at local hospitals as well as painting his own self-portrait, as a clown, and then (b) murdering thirty-three boys and burying them under his house. He dedicated his life to becoming a case in point.

Interestingly, phobias almost never arise from smell or sound, at least in humans. Disgusted by poo, yes, but phobic, no. Appalled by the sound of Britney Spears, certainly, but no compulsion to run away in panic unless you're Avril Lavigne. It's different for animals. My dog has a phobia of me biting into a McIntosh apple. When I do this, he streaks out of the room as if his tail is on fire. Don't ask me why he tolerates the sound of a chewed-on carrot. I'd chalk that one up to Roger Callahan's random perturbance. Wouldn't you?

EFFORTS AT ESCAPE

La Dentista

The other day I was in Mexico, puttering about content-edly as I shopped for market silver and fantasized about buying a villa, when all of a sudden my tooth burst into the sensory equivalent of the helicopters roaring onto the beach in *Apocalypse Now*, with Wagner blasting from loud-speakers, the sound of gunfire, and everyone screaming on the ground.

"Don't worry about it," I muttered to my travelling companion over breakfast, chewing pan dulce on the other side of my mouth and clutching my jaw while seeing stars every time I sipped my hot coffee. "I'll be fine."

Of course, this is what you say when you are in a small mountain village in central Mexico and you have no interest, WHATSOEVER, in seeking out a dentist on the unpaved main street, where dengue fever is warned of in posters peeling from adobe walls and all the dogs are three-legged.

"I'll just take some Advil," I added, holding my head very still. Twelve hours later I had run out of all the avail-able Advil in the town of Tepoztlán, and was crawling around a suburb in the nearby city of Cuernavaca, with an address for *la dentista* in my hand, written on the back of a hotel envelope by the hotel manager's wife. Apparently, the wife had advised the manager that one of their patrons had been spotted with a dining room napkin wrapped around her jaw and tied at the top of her head in a bow. The manager told the front desk clerk, and she put me in touch with the dentist by telephone.

Unfortunately, owing to my inability to speak passable Spanish and the dentist's reciprocal inability to speak English, all I knew for certain was the time of my appointment. I was fairly sure, however, that the dentist had said, before hanging up: "We don't use drills here. We only use powder and air."

Thus I found myself nagged forward through the dark and confusing residential streets of Cuernavaca by my curiosity as much as my pain. "What the *hell* kind of dentistry involves the deployment of powder and air?"

At last my companion and I found the right house, walled in and barb-wired like all of the other compounds in this posh neighbourhood, suggesting that Mexico City's crime wave had lapped over the volcanic ridges that surround the capital, enclosing its outrageous pollution, and spilled into this smaller metropolis forty-five minutes away. After a spell of anxious silence, a maid let us through the ten-foot gate, then down a cobbled drive lined with flowering forsythia, and into a reception area on the side of the white stone house. She flipped on the light and nodded shyly, indicating that we were to wait. We bided our time with Latino celebrity magazines—a spread of photos of Julio Iglesias's daughter's wedding; gossip about who amid Mexico's Who's Who had taken a bribe.

Fifteen minutes elapsed in this quiet white-washed room, and then the dentist suddenly poked her head in. She was a petite woman in glasses with a bob of chestnut hair. She apologized for her tardiness, explaining that her children were a handful this evening because of the excitement of la Dia de los Muertes, or the Mexican Day of the Dead. I wondered why she had agreed to see me at all, under the circumstances, but was in no mood to politely protest.

La dentista ushered me into a dimly lit room that boasted one dental chair and an instrument table. The paint was peeling off the ceiling, I noticed when I was made to recline. There weren't any model teeth sitting on shelves or brochures for bleaching procedures, or framed Monet posters on the walls. Much less cupboards or an assistant. On the other hand, there was no lite rock playing from hidden wall speakers, either. Think of that. To have your teeth drilled without the sonic accompaniment of *NSync is a brilliant innovation in dentistry, in my view. On the other hand, the ambience was such that the torture scene from *Marathon Man* did flash through my mind as I stretched my mouth wide. (Perhaps you'll recall that film, in which Dustin Hoffman has his teeth drilled without anaesthetic, one after the other, by a mad dentist in an empty warehouse until he confesses to not flossing.)

"Do you have dollars?" *la dentista* asked. I shook my

head no. She tapped my troubled tooth experimentally and I yelped. This seemed to surprise her. "Sorry," she murmured. In retrospect, I realized that she had not asked me if I had dollars. She had asked me if I had pain: *dolor.* Now, she was proceeding on the assumption that I had neither dollars nor pain, which perhaps accounts for what she did next.

By listening to her queries and guessing at the meaning of her hand gestures, I soon figured out the words for "open" and "shut," and this made matters worse, for it encouraged her to think that I understood Spanish perfectly and was on the verge of translating the works of Cervantes. She stopped trying to speak English altogether. No need!

"La bla bla de bla bla, tonces, bla bla-ista, si?" she asked.

"Okay," I said, after a long, frog-mouthed pause.

She fired up a drill and began shaving off the tops of all my fillings, for reasons that she had probably just explained but that eluded me entirely. In truth, they continue to elude me to this day, those reasons, but at the time, all I was thinking was: "*Please* don't let her hit a nerve, please, please."

After ten minutes of paring down all of my teeth, she stopped and put on a pair of sunglasses. "La bla bla de bla bla. Claro Patricia?"

I gave a noncommittal nod.

She whipped out a batonlike object, flipped on a switch, and began to pass the baton slowly back and forth along my lower jaw. It made no sound. It never touched me. Just slowly waved back and forth. Well, I thought to myself, that's what I would do if someone interrupted my Dia de los Muertes celebrations and had neither dollars nor pain. Remove their fillings and wave a wand over their head. Then I had an epiphany. Aha: the powder and air. When I spoke with her on the phone, she must have said POWER and air, which must have meant air-powered air, or . . . maybe . . . power in the air. That was it. Power in the air.

"Laser," she explained, reading my expression. "The laser will calm your dollars for now until your *dentisto* at home can do the work necessary."

She was a LASER dentist, you see, not primitive at all. On the contrary, very cutting edge. What a first-world snob I had been. This kind of dentistry has been practised for only ten years or so. According to the Canadian Dental Association, lasers have a number of useful roles in dentistry, none of which relate to what the Cuernavaca dentist did to my mouth. But lasers can be used in root surface treatment, the treatment of gingivitis, to strengthen tooth enamel, and to seal fissures or sterilize the site of orthodontic work.

"Dentists should be properly trained in the use of this equipment," the CDA warns in its official position on laser dentistry, "because of the inherent risk connected with its improper use. Educational requirements for the use of lasers in dental offices and facilities should be such that proper and safe use of this equipment is assured, and should include theoretical training, clinical training, and a meaningful examination to ensure competence."

I quote that in order to reassure readers that wand waving is not taken lightly here in Canada.

At any rate, by sheer and staggering coincidence, two days after I saw the dentist in Cuernavaca, I woke up with my face so swollen on one side that I appeared to have elephantiasis. As a matter of fact, it was possible that I did have elephantiasis because, why not?

At breakfast, mouthing pan dulce and slurping coffee, my travel companion and I went through the same conversation.

"Are you all right?"

"I'm fine. Just need some Advil."

The garden in which we were seated was exquisite. Lush green lawns faced the sheer cliffs of the Tepozteco volcanic range, where one could see an ancient Aztec temple atop a ridge. Fountains burbled. Flowers bloomed. Music played, dreamy and quiet. Alas, owing to Post-Tramautic Stress Disorder, I would never return.

An hour later I was in the local health clinic, which was deserted on Sunday at church time except for *la doctora*, a calm, quiet woman in jeans who led me into a clean examination room and beheld my face without alarm. *El elephantisio* was now differentially diagnosed as *una problema con su dentista*. My jaw was infected, she suggested, and it would take some time for the swelling to abate.

This was deeply disturbing, for a number of reasons, including the fact that I'd planned to reconnect on this holiday with a long-lost love, who would now bring new meaning to the phrase "Why, you've *changed*."

"Things are different, now, Patricia," I could imagine him saying, "we're different. I'm married now, a father. And your left eye has disappeared from view behind a fold of skin."

I contemplated this scenario as I bent over with my pants down and *la doctora* injected steroids into my bum. She also gave me a prescription for Cipro, arguably a more suitable antibiotic for anthrax contamination than dental infections, but it did the trick. Particularly when combined with *cerveza*, it had the salutary effect of making me decide to rent a house in the town and move my family to Mexico for six months.

In my next dispatch from the frontiers of thoroughly ruined holidays: why, if you have two small children, a dog, and three cats, you should not inhabit a villa that was lovingly designed, furnished, and landscaped by two gay architects from Acapulco.

A Simpler Life at Casa Patsy

"You're going to *Mexico* for six months?"

This, generally, the astonished question one gets from friends when one announces that one is going to Mexico for six months. Depending upon the friend, the word emphasis might change, from "you're going to *Mexico*?" to "you're going to Mexico for six *months*?"—with one or two people locating their adamant incredulity squarely on the "*you're* going," as in "you, *Patricia Pearson*, are going to Mexico for six months?"

The only reason I can imagine that going to Mexico for six months is so surprising is because most of my friends are parents now and tend to assume that they have signed their lives over to an international consortium of petting zoos.

But, I try to tell them, I have a quest. I am blowing a gasket and I need to find simplicity. Go away media. Go away malls and pop-up ads and choices and false expertise. Shoo. I want to move to a wild, rugged, and beautiful place that is warm and languid, with no Fox TV or SUVs. Where my children can be exposed to village life, to the importance of community ritual, to the reality of poverty. Where they can discover a world wholly unfamiliar with John Ritter's last hurrah as the voice of Clifford the Big Red Dog.

"But why Mexico?" the friends ask, as if Canada's boreal forest would do.

The idea of going to Mexico came to me when I was reading a newspaper in Starbucks one day and discovered that the Mexican government had changed its laws on citizenship. It used to be that if you had Mexican citizenship, you could not carry a passport from any other country. *Viva Mexico!* Thus, although I was born in Mexico City, when my father was posted there, I had to renounce Mexican citizenship at the age of twenty-one in order to remain a Canadian. In 1998, however—as I was discovering in the newspaper over a vanilla latte—the Mexican government repealed this law, primarily in order to encourage Mexican émigrés to the United States to move freely back and forth and to invest their dollars back home. *Ay caramba!* In their wake—surprise!—came me.

Needless to say, the daughter of a Canadian diplomat was not the intended beneficiary of the law, but I'm harmless enough. And it was my birthright. After all, I came into the world hearing muttered Spanish and was first held by Mexican hands. *"Una niña!"* was the very first observation made about me. I was conceived, conceptualized, and announced in Mexico. What could be more fitting than a return to my first hurrah?

My bid for serenity began in a snowstorm at five in the morning after a sleepless night of worrying that I would sleep through my alarm, compounded by even more extreme worry that I would never fall asleep at all. Which indeed I did not. Among the many useless notions that blundered like fat drunks at a frat house party through my mind all that night was that, if I ever wished to deprive Ambrose of sleep, in order to more effectively interrogate him about where he left the car keys, I could just tell him that he had to catch a flight at six on the following morning. Really, this is all one need do—to spouses, or prisoners of war. You don't have to be inhumane. Simply tell your captive that they have an escape opportunity at dawn on the following day, but that no one will be available to wake them up. Nothing works better.

I finally lurched out of bed vibrating with stress before the alarm went off, and next faced the quandary of having to trudge through foot-deep snow in my ready-for-Mexico running shoes as I swept my car free of its new white winter coat. The drive to the airport, in blowing snow with fishtail slush on the highway, was raggedly tense. I felt bitterly jealous of Ambrose, still warmly asleep in the house, who was scheduled to come a few days later with the children. If a blue fairy had appeared just then, warm and affectionate and confident like the fairy in *Pinocchio*, and said, "What is your wish?" I would have said, "Bed."

But she didn't appear, and when I parked at the drop-off lot, snow billowing around me in the darkness, I encountered two men engaged in irritable verbal fisticuffs, fuck you—no, fuck you—fuck this. Kevin climbed into the airport shuttle with me, and the woman behind us bellowed, "Oh for *God's* sake, a dog," as if Kevin were the last straw. We all proceeded in hostile silence to the terminal.

Deliver me please, God, from Canada in January at dawn. From a people disheartened by weather and darkness and SARS and the prospect of war.

Seven hours later, warm as toast in my ski jacket, I found Kevin's cage at the Mexico City airport amid pieces of luggage. He cried with relief when he heard my voice. I didn't need Rochelle Gai Rodney to discern what he was thinking. After he recovered from the shock of flying cargo, followed by an hour in a minivan on hairpin mountain roads as we steered clear of Mexico City and went over the volcanic rim to Tepoztlán, Kevin turned into Jack in *The Nightmare Before Christmas:* What's this? What's this? What smell do I find here? What's this, a donkey on the ro-oad. What's this? Horse poo? And there! A cat with one le-eg. What's this, a swimming pool for meee?"

My dog explored while I, exhausted, sat at the long wooden table in my open-air dining room, gazing out at a large garden filled with the cactus, hibiscus, and plum trees that encircled our swimming pool. Beyond the garden lay a wild valley full of honeysuckle and magnolia trees. Or, that probably wasn't right—more likely it was forsythia and mango trees. Or jasmine and pine trees. Actually, I didn't have a goddamn clue what I was looking at, but it was pretty and it smelled nice.

Raising my gaze, I found myself staring at a jagged

hill—bare and craggy at its summit. The hill was close enough to shoot at, if one were so inclined, and thus we would come to watch the vultures who nested there and who otherwise wheeled noiselessly above us, waiting for one of our pets to be poisoned by the landlord. About which more later.

On very clear days, from our bedroom balcony we can see Mexico's largest active volcano, the magnificent Popocatepetl, which is an ancient Nahuatl word meaning "we don't much care for vowels." The volcano is perfectly cone-shaped. From its tip streams an extraordinary plume of steam and gas because Popocatepetl is volatile these days, and keenly watched by volcanologists.

When Ambrose and the children arrived, we settled into an extremely basic routine. Geoffrey wandered around naked, placing his Carnegie Collection dinosaurs at various strategic posts in the shrubbery, while Clara and the dog swam in the pool, and Ambrose came down with some combination of malaria, Ebola, and dengue fever, retreating to the bedroom, never to be seen again. I wrote stuff, and followed news on the Internet about the Bush administration's mounting impatience with the rest of the world for their failure to see the threat from Iraq. The Security Council needs to "stand up and be counted," I remember Condi Rice saying, as if all of its members, which included Mexico at the time, were cowering and blubbering like "girlie men" rather than offering valid objections to a hurried and precipitous invasion.

Unsettled, I walked down into town to read the Mexican

papers that are sold in the square and found myself gazing in wonder at a magazine cover that featured a fat naked man slumped over dead on his toilet. This was a true crime magazine. These are extremely popular in Mexico, so don't get the idea that a people committed to family, community, and church aren't also fond of seeing fat naked men dead on toilets, because they are.

Indeed, I would be remiss if I suggested that there was less sensationalism or clamour in Mexico. It is just that their ruckus is different. On a typical morning in Tepoztlán for instance, you awaken not to telemarketers, pundits, and TV ads, but to an incessant overlay of barking dogs, backfiring trucks, squealing pigs, chirping crickets, crowing roosters, clanging brass bands, and exploding firecrackers. By midafternoon, I might add, when most other noises have calmed down, the firecrackers are still going off all over the arid highly incendiary landscape. They are meant to scare off the devil, and maybe they do. The also cause me to poke myself in the eye with my mascara brush. Sundays, naturally, are the worst. Ash Wednesday through Easter are insufferable.

The town of Tepoztlán has been written up by anthropologists as a classic Mexican pueblo. It is where the famously drunken author Malcolm Lowry situated *Under the Volcano*, his brilliant novel about a diplomat's self-destruction through drink. I could certainly see the route to excessive drinking here, with tequila for sale in all of the corner stores, and corner stores the preferred business venture of the citizenry, who simply knock off their living room walls to proffer tomatillos, Cheetos, and booze. The trouble is that getting to a corner store from our place involved a steep ankle-twisting cobblestone walk downhill past packs of matted wild dogs and starved sullen cows, with roosters hopping sideways to avoid the hurtling taxis and *collectivos*, vehicles that stir up a dust so thick it renders your pants unrecognizable.

"Honey," I might announce to the prone and perspiring Ambrose, "I'm just gonna trip and limp to the corner store after I change into my rubber overalls and spray myself with Cow Be Gone, do you remember where you put the Fuck Off Scary Dog repellent?"

And then off I'd go, returning about an hour later, red-faced from heat exhaustion, prepared to quaff the entire six-pack of Modelo beer that I'd just purchased on the spot.

The siesta, you must know, is a classic Mexican pueblo ritual, invented to sleep off the beer and sunstroke entailed in one's initial foray to the corner store, or office or factory or what have you, before daring to resume the rest of one's daily affairs. Interestingly, the Mexicans possessed no livestock whatsoever before the arrival of the Spanish conquistadors in the sixteenth century, which means that they owned neither mules nor horses and had to go everywhere on foot. I'm fairly certain that this would have left them red-faced, exhausted, and drunk at least once a day, and I'm not entirely surprised to learn that the average lifespan in that time was twenty-seven years. After that, their feet were just blistered stumps and they had to lie down.

We in more northern climes should rethink our roman-
ticization of the siesta and, while we are at it, stop pining
for the spa and the pedicure. A simpler life begins by
counting one's blessings.

The Neighbours in the Shrubbery

Can blessings include a car?

I've been wondering about this because a simple life can actually get rather complicated when the nearest decent supermarket is twenty-five kilometres away. Granted we flew down thinking in terms of margaritas and tranquillity, with some vague idea of home schooling lamely tacked on to the fantasy, but after seventeen trips to the farmer's market to buy as many boxes of Cheerios and juice as could fit in our knapsacks while we puffed and gasped uphill to our mountain retreat, we began thinking: No. Not quite right. We need a car. A car for bulk shopping and stray-horse protection and for . . . making the children go away! This latter thought occurs after a spell of non-stop shrieking that suggests that my children need a more concrete routine.

Car. School. Car. School. Car. More beer. Some tequila. School.

This, my mantra in the meditative ambience of Tepoztlán.

We quickly locate car and school, and I am transformed into a mutant suburban mom, driving the kids to their petite Beatrix Potterish *escuela* in our newly acquired and irredeemably ancient 1989 Chrysler Shadow, popping into the Superama for Fruit Roll-ups and beer, dashing into the Woolworth's in Cuernavaca for piñata supplies, before returning to my idyllic house in order to hastily become an author contemplating the universe under the volcano, after which I jump back into the Shadow and scoot back to school to be this week's volunteer parent at the dog-neutering drive.

Lest I feel overwhelmed, I have noticed a poster in town advertising a Friday afternoon meeting for Neurotics Anonymous. I am tempted to go, if only to discover whether they have merely misspelled "narcotics." But, the truth is, I don't feel tense, for it isn't like that. There are arrangements to be made, and loud bangs driving mascara wands into my eye, but there aren't any choices. Tepoztlán has only one bilingual school. The end. We met one person who had a car for sale. Here's your dough. We don't know a soul, so there goes the need for a datebook in which to pencil in lunch dates. We receive no phone calls. Ever. We never have mail. There are no billboards. We possess no TV. There is little public sanctimony and even less health hysteria. Geoffrey stands in the car as I drive. We crack open cans of Modelo beer as we walk. Kevin can poo on the street, and nobody cares if we don't have a baggie, this being a town where untended animals outnumber people by a factor of two to one.

Despondent, as I sometimes am, when I feel homesick or worried about world affairs and head lice, I step fully dressed into the swimming pool, my dress floating up above my body as I sink in the cool water. The spontaneity of this limpid gesture cheers me up, and I tiptoe-walk through the chest-high water, engaged in the rescue of drowning butterflies.

Mexico has changed since the 1960s, when my mother still remembers going into a restaurant bathroom and finding, for toilet paper, a box of spoiled ballots. But it hasn't changed that much. There is a Wal-Mart in nearby Cuernavaca and a flourishment of Internet cafés in Tepoztlán, as well as some highly sophisticated restaurants and shops catering to the Mexico City weekenders. But, on the whole, materialism and status consciousness have not yet insinuated themselves as a dominant value. Nor—for better or worse—has political debate beyond the sophisticated circles in urban centres.

"What do you think of the Americans invading Iraq?" I asked one taxi driver who spoke English. He considered the question, tilting his head, knitting his brows, and then after lengthy reflection, he answered me with a slight apologetic shrug of his shoulders: "Nothing."

The taxi drivers play penny poker on the hoods of their VW bugs and affably but resignedly allow us to interrupt them with a fare, ferrying us along the cobblestones with crucifixes and Smurfs swaying madly from their rearviews.

When we walk along our road, called Camino San Juan, friendly women chat with us from their half-completed cinder-block houses in the brambles. I have no idea what we and they are discussing, but gestures and warm smiles suffice. What is compelling and unusual about the town, as I think on it now, is that the barriers aren't as pronounced—between inside and outside, work and family, self and community, life and death, weekend and weekday, rich and poor, nature and civilization. There is a sense, however difficult to measure, of being connected to everything vital around you.

In the evening we often wend our way up San Juan as the sun begins to edge toward the horizon. The warm light thrown upon the cliffs above us and to the east is stunning, like the suffused reds and rusts of the Grand Canyon. Clara might find a horseshoe or a dead snake— and, once, a puppy that we brought home. Geoffrey collects fallen hibiscus petals. Kevin wanders into the corner store proprietor's living room, behind the racks of candy and scarfs down the cat's food.

Life has a fluid immediacy, that preoccupies and consoles.

Some Thoughts on Being an Immigrant

Recently I have been pondering the function of language in an immigrant's life. Shortly before I left for Mexico, I had an opportunity to speak to some New Canadians—which is what Old Canadians who work for the government call immigrants nowadays, in our revised political rhetoric—and they told me about how difficult the transition can be, from living as an Old Yugoslavian or Old Rwandan or what have you to becoming a New Canadian.

The gist of this dinner party conversation was that being a New Canadian can be highly alarming, notwithstanding the fact that many Old Canadians perceive New Canadians to be living indolently and contentedly off of the welfare state. But no, say the New Canadians, in fact they are often humiliated to find themselves back at square one, driving cabs or selling fruit, getting lost and stammering apologies in broken English. They hasten to add that they are grateful for the refuge and the freedom, but much is displaced in exile, including one's basic sense of competence.

Maybe I understood abstractly what they were getting

at, but now that I am in Mexico the lightbulb has been really switched on. *Ding.*

"*Señora!*" exclaimed the big grinning customs officer at the airport upon my arrival. "How can j'hou be Mexicana? You don' even speak *Español!*"

Well, true. I tried to tell him that I'd forgotten how, but I couldn't remember the Spanish word for *forget.*

I do know some vocabulary, but it tends to come out as an inscrutable mixture of Spanish, French, and stutter. I recently inquired of a fellow Mexican: "*Qu'est que c'est la palabra por . . . uh . . . por . . . uh . . . conoce* Scotch tape?"

This was actually, technically, a trilingual sentence, which ought to have earned me some points, except that it managed to project what New Canadians would call an aura of rank stupidity. Language is a major obstacle, in this sense, because until you are fluent you cannot surmount people's perceptions of you as really kinda dumb. The identity crisis is swift and merciless. In a matter of days, you go from being an eloquent and confident person to a goof in a clown suit with foot-long shoes.

Today I answered a question in the affirmative by conflating French and Spanish and saying *s'oui,* which would be tantamount to a New Canadian saying "yesh," as if they'd just slurped up half a dozen shooters. And the listener cannot help it: When somebody says "yesh" or "*s'oui,*" you think they're inebriated, disabled, or mildly insane. I know this for a fact because one night after I returned to Toronto, I was in a bar when a young Mexican man from the town of Toluca, ironically not far from

Tepoztlán, asked to join me. I said no, I'm working, but he joined me anyway and wanted me to know that he was an architect by training, even if he was just now working in a restaurant.

"It is difficult to have aspirations here," he said. Then he raised his hand in the universal gesture of stop, to command my attention. "Consider: what is your definition of asthma?"

"Asthma?" I repeated, uncertain.

"Asthma." He nodded solemnly.

"A breathing condition," I ventured.

"Exactly," he said, and he lifted his baseball cap, ran a hand through his hair, then replaced the cap, sighing. "I only dream in the day. This is the problem."

No, amigo, that's only one of the problems.

There are occasions when I say things that I am convinced are perfectly correct, in Spanish, yet for some reason they still elicit uproarious belly laughs. In puzzlement, I try to deconstruct my errors afterward with my dictionary. This is how I realized that when I wanted to go horseback riding one afternoon, I inadvertently announced my need to hire an onion, while on another day the casual assertion to a cab driver that I would show him where I wanted to go was, in fact, the declaration: "I am monstrous."

There is an upside to this quandary, though, which is that you lose all vestige of your own prejudices about people, because without command of the language, you are completely undiscerning. You can get along famously with absolutely anyone, be they oaf or Nobel laureate.

I had an incredibly engaging conversation with a local cactus farmer, days after the death of Maurice Gibb of the Bee Gees, whose music this man was playing in memoriam, on a tinny radio hung from a jacaranda tree. I was so stimulated by the task of figuring out the past tense of *die*—as in, "it's so sad that Maurice Gibb DIED," rather than "it is very tragic that Maurice Gibb deaded," or "what a shame that Maurice Gibb will have deathed"— that the farmer might as well have been Noam Chomsky forcing me to defend my position on the fallacy of global activism at the grassroots level rather than a sun-wizened man in a worn sombrero, squinting in the light and waiting patiently as I struggled to avoid saying, "Hello, I am monstrous. What a sadness that your singer has died-ed."

A Word About Ambition

Today, as a New Mexican, I've been thinking about the downward slide of ambition in an immigrant's life. It is often said that immigrants are ambitious to provide a better life for their children. But what about themselves? New Canadians have told me about how they get bogged down in the challenges of an unfamiliar landscape and take years to feel free enough to pursue loftier goals. I understand that now. The abstract daydreamy ambition I entertained all the time in Canada has been distilled in Mexico into a very modest and specific ambition not to inadvertently plow my car into a herd of cows.

Of course, I also try to avoid donkeys, schoolchildren, possums, and piles of rubble as I rattle along in a sedan that can no longer drive over a green pea without juddering. The roads here are cobbled together with large chunks of volcanic rock, which means that driving the children to school involves clambering over terrain that is so marvellously bad it wouldn't be fit for a Humvee, let alone a Chrysler Shadow that regularly stalls and casts off parts.

Due to the conditions, all Tepoztlán traffic progresses at

the pace of minus ten kilometres an hour, with cars creeping all over the road to find the least-menacing chunk to ease over before they arrive, every two blocks or so, at the SPEED BUMPS that some authority ordered built—I assume—for the purpose of bolstering a nephew's struggling cement business.

For no particular reason, one sometimes comes across an actual paved stretch of road, which all drivers immediately zoom over like supercharged Indy racers, causing the aforementioned dog collisions. In any event, the whole process of "commuting," which in Canada provided time for rumination, was now as demanding of my concentration as a pinball game. The same proved true for cafés. What better place to write, daydream, and scheme than a café, you might ask. But I was dealing with this ridiculous sort of *Groundhog Day* problem in the local café, wherein I would go in and order a café Americano, and the woman served it to me black, and I had to wait for her to be free again—periodically flailing my arm in the air—so that I could request milk, which she would, at length, bring over with this pointed expression on her face, so that I'd spend the rest of my time wondering what she was thinking. Some weeks went by before I realized that café Americano in Mexico just means black coffee.

Once I had slapped myself on the forehead and sorted out that problem, I turned my attention to figuring out what a Mexican centime was worth and whether or not I owed a tip, and if so how much extra for tormenting waitresses by repeatedly ordering black coffee and then asking for milk.

A Polish friend of mine remembers that he spent a solid eighteen months when he first arrived in Canada just trying to figure out what people were talking about in the *Globe and Mail*. Another friend was so baffled by urban transit signs that she became agoraphobic. A third got so bedevilled by the lack of familiar reference points that he had a panic attack, which he mistook for a coronary. When the paramedics came, he later told me, they checked his vitals and then asked him how long he'd been in the country. Apparently, this happened a lot.

Being unable to take the ground beneath one's feet for granted is a major impediment to being ambitious. Multi-tasking is definitely out. I used to be able to walk with my toddler, for instance, and take a cellphone call. Here, my eyes are frantically peeled for scorpions, donkey shit, and mongrels. Consider every parent's warning to their toddler about not touching strange dogs. In Mexico, the dogs all look like a canine version of Pigpen in *Peanuts*, lost in a swirl of dust as they slink along the littered underbrush on the sides of the roads. If one of them gets hit by a speeding taxi, the others act as if they've found an all-you-can-eat buffet.

Thus, telling a toddler not to pat the doggie roughly translates into this: Geoffrey, get back from the snarling, half-starved, germ-infested cannibal. He might not be in a good mood.

Puppies pose a particular dilemma because you don't

want your child to think that a puppy couldn't be an angel, but when I hesitated for a long moment when Clara wanted to play with one, a Mexican mother came up to me and said: "What does your daughter want?" I think that's what she said. Maybe she said: "Shame about our soccer heroes losing to those dirty-pig Argentinians, don't you agree?" At any rate, I replied in Spanish: "She wants to play the dog like a violin," which wasn't what I meant. The *señora* looked at me as if I was insane and made it clear that only bad, reckless mothers hesitate about letting children approach stray dogs.

Soon enough one craves the familiar, if only to boost one's confidence in small decision making. So it is that finding a frozen package of McCain Superfries in the Cuernavaca Superama elicits a ludicrous cry of delight. *I know what these taste like and how to make them!*

This is why immigrants establish their Little Indias and Chinatowns and so forth—because they need a little corner of the world that isn't baffling. To that end, I'm thinking of establishing a Little Canada here in the town of Tepoztlán.

It could be like a block-long neighbourhood where nobody makes eye contact or says anything loud, and all the stores have huge blocks of cheddar hanging in the windows, with bins outside full of maple fudge and President's Choice "Memories of Butter" brand margarine. You'd walk inside the stores, and they'd all have black-and-white TVs behind the counters tuned to the Air Farce, with a space beside the Royal Bank ATM along the back wall for an air hockey table. At the Beaver Hut Diner, you'd find framed pictures of the owner posing with Céline Dion or with Michael Ignatieff in a tilted sombrero. "Fabulous tuna casserole" would be scrolled on the picture, along with the celebrity's signature. During the World Cup, all the Canadian-Mexicans could gather in Little Canada to watch Wimbledon or have a health care debate.

And so ends the story of how Patricia Pearson, writer and journalist, became the satisfied proprietress of a cheese shop in Mexico.

Serenity with a Full Complement of Spies

Lately I have been spending mornings at a language school, in order to improve my ability to fight with my landlord, who has been evincing an odd, anal-retentive approach to his plants. I sit at a plastic patio table beneath an orange tree with my instructor, a faintly mustachioed, sandal-clad linguist named Sylvia who runs her small school like an extended family barbecue, with her boyfriend, her son, and a cousin on staff, and an elderly mother who can often be found weeping soundlessly about widowhood in a corner of the office. In between exasperated arguments with her relations and frantic attempts to organize field trips for twenty schoolboys from Denver, Sylvia has been teaching me how to say to Fernando: "What do you mean, you're charging me twenty-five pesos for a stepped-on plant?"

I have always been deeply uncomfortable with land-lords because they make me feel self-conscious, as if I'm about to get in trouble but can never predict for what. This self-consciousness in turn leads to all manner of curious predicaments. Once, in college, my landlord came into my apartment to check on some plumbing while I was sound asleep, buried under my duvet. Given that it was noon, and he had no reason to expect me to be in, he was unaware of my presence on the futon, when he sat down on it to make a phone call, placing his rear end approximately four inches from my face. Now this is one of those situations that you simply cannot get out of unless you act swiftly.

Crucial minutes passed, in which I was too shocked and embarrassed to reveal myself to the landlord, and then my chance to sing out gaily "Oh, excuse me!" was lost forever. One does not lie for five minutes with one's nose next to a near-stranger's bum and then suddenly emit an airy exclamation. There was nothing for it but to lie deathly still, barely breathing and praying to God that my landlord held his position and didn't sit on my head.

After two and a half centuries, he finished his phone conversation and left, and I vowed to myself that I would buy a house as soon as I possibly could.

A happy decade followed, before I re-entered the humiliating realm of the tenant.

Relations began amiably with Fernando, of course, when we first arrived—no hint yet that he suspected us of rank vandalism. Early on, he and his partner invited us over to lunch. Their house bordered ours, and they seemed to have developed both properties as a dream project, an infatuated meeting of two lovers' minds—Fernando being an architect and Philip a landscape designer. It never seems to have crossed their minds that a house with real inhabitants might bring them rental income, true, but RUIN EVERYTHING.

We first felt a faint breeze of dissonance when we went to lunch at the appointed hour of two and noticed that they lived a remarkably clutter-free existence in a round gabled home with sparse furniture, few objects, and perfect floral arrangements. At first I wondered if they'd hidden their stuff, preparing for a photo spread in *Architectural Digest* or something, but I eventually learned that they were not the sort of people who owned any stuff, lest the stuff impinge upon the aesthetic of walls and floors and gardens. Philip, the landscape architect, was a grandfather from Maine with a thick, drooping moustache and easy smile. He favoured short cut-off jeans and flip-flops, and seemed happiest puttering amongst his prize tropical flora, with a packet of cigarettes hanging precariously out of his dress-shirt pocket. I cannot recall how he hooked up with Fernando, a patrician architect with aquiline features and a silver beard, who sported white linen shirts, sleeves rolled up, and chinos. But they were clearly a smitten couple.

The pair had a fine, glossy-coated Rottweiler named Luna who tended to amble over to our side of the bamboo gates and scarf down large wheels of Oaxaca cheese grabbed straight off the table. You could hear Luna at night in her pen, her deep, gulping Rottweiler bark providing a base note to the squeals of terrified pigs at the slaughterhouse across the road. At first, we felt we had pet ownership in common, what with Luna and Kevin smelling each other's bums on a daily basis. But it soon grew apparent that, in addition to being a consummate cheese thief, Luna's job was to pure-breed puppies and to serve as a cheap alarm system. She never went for walks, received little attention, and wasn't permitted inside their house under any circumstances. Indeed, it would have been insanely unthinkable, like inviting a cow into Tiffany's. Thus the seeds of Fernando's exasperation with us were germinating.

Fernando generally resided in an elegant home in Acapulco, having been raised as an upper-class *rico* in the Yucatán. When he wished to communicate with us, he spurned email or the telephone in favour of dispatching Mario the gardener or Abondia the maid, with a note written on embossed stationery. At lunch, he and Philip served paella. It was a neighbourhood guest list, to intro-duce us to people of merit on Camino San Juan. Not the neighbours who lived in the shrubbery, but the nattily attired sociologist from down the road and the health food entrepreneur from Mexico City who chain-smoked, and a smattering of other relaxed yet elegant folk for whom Tepoztlán was a weekend getaway. They all imbibed red wine followed by cocktails as they lounged, first on the veranda and then on the lawn, in the long, boozy luncheon style of Mexicans. The Gatsby-esque atmosphere was charming, yet also impossible, really, for us to partake in after the orange soda ran out. Geoffrey began digging in the flower bed with his dessert spoon.

Inasmuch as our own sophistication ended abruptly where our dog and two children began, it seemed a matter of necessity to conceal this very fact from Philip and Fernando. What is the point, they might well ask each other angrily, of furnishing a swimming pool patio with white-cushioned chaise longues if the cushions are destined to be covered in small children's footprints? Why on earth import a rare cactus and place it just so in a desert garden if it merely lures a little girl armed with craft scissors? And the pool itself—the spare, turquoise "splash pool," as Mexicans call the foreshortened, shallow-ledged pools in which they enjoyed double shots of Jimador—how could it be so boorishly despoiled?

I was helpless where the pool was concerned—I do have to say that in my own defence. For Geoffrey began running a continual science experiment designed to address the abiding query of the (two-year-old) human mind: What floats? What sinks? On any given morning, particularly when Geoffrey had gone about his experiments after dark and escaped notice, the pool contained what appeared to be the entire contents of a yard sale, replete with espresso maker, stegosaurus, wooden spoons, tea bags, my bra, and anything prized by Clara, in particular Penelope, the battery-operated talking dragon. I constantly apologized to Mario, whom I'd find early in the morning, stoically and gracefully fishing the yard sale contents out with his pole, bent over the water in the one T-shirt he owned, his olive-skinned arms reaching for waterlogged toys and submerged barbecue tongs as he lived out the theme of a Luis Buñuel film without comment.

Every now and then he would glance up at me and smile shyly, a beautiful young man with the classic features of a Nahuatl Indian, high-boned and almond-eyed, his hair dark as onyx. Little did I know that Mario was dutifully reporting back to Fernando about our transgressions, acting as an undercover operative who had infiltrated tenant lines.

Landlords are not supposed to know what tenants get up to until tenants leave, said tenants having madly scrubbed and polished the premises to leave no trace of their lives. Landlords remain blissfully ignorant, provided their tenants aren't engaging in serial murder or pet hoarding. (As I write, a woman in Wisconsin has just been evicted for keeping seventy-six ducks in her apartment. It is this sort of person, this sort of owner of seventy-six ducks, whom I wish Diane Sawyer would interview with that concerned and puzzled knit to her brows. "Why seventy-*six* ducks?") Anyway, in Mexico, the rules are different. You get to be spied upon every single day by the "gardener" and also by the "maid." It is said here that the walls have ears, a situation compounded by the striking absence of physical walls, so that said gardener and maid can observe you eating dinner in your dining room, and watch you cooking quesadillas in the kitchen and file eyewitness reports of your six-year-old using the antique chest of drawers as a nest for the blind and hairless newborn opossum she has found ejected from its dead mother's pouch on the side of the road.

Thus it was that Fernando dropped by one afternoon with a pool maintenance man and explained to me with a tight and condescending cheerfulness that pools filled with appliances and toys tended to run up filtration repair bills, which naturally I would be expected to pay.

His greatest angst, however, arose over the treatment of Philip's plants. This was a predicament to which I was doomed when I rented the house on the Day of the Dead with a swollen head and a hangover, and not the faintest passing acquaintance with the difference between rhododendrons and thistles. I had never noticed the plants at all, and I first realized Fernando's anguish because of Kevin. My dog has a psychotic habit of nosing large stones around and then chewing and snapping anxiously at the grass surrounding the stone, as if frantically attempting to free it from its grass . . . trap? . . . before the stone, or "egg," perhaps, or "small, hard, inert puppy" is . . . killed? By cats? Or captured by the enemy? In any event, Kevin has been doing this all his life, and it was never more than just ridiculous behaviour until the grass belonged to Philip and Fernando. Then it became the source of whispers, rumours, mounting tension, and finally a note on embossed stationery: Kevin was to be tied up.

Shocked, for the lawn was mostly perfect, as Kevin rarely finds the right sort of (sacred? egglike?) stone to set him off, I considered pointing out to Fernando that the issue here was just a bunch of fucking grass. Happy, easygoing, growable grass, versus a dog free to move more than five feet in any direction. But I held my tongue and even let it plague me with acute self-consciousness, finding myself rushing at Kevin and squawking like a frenzied hen to make him stop it, stop it! until one afternoon, noting that we had refused to tether our dog, Fernando upped the ante. I was furnished with a bill for 250 pesos "for the plant that was destroyed."

This ominous and entirely ambiguous note was delivered via Mario, and offered no further elaboration, as if I knew exactly what plant was meant because I had just had a thunderous party at which several large men got hammered and crashed over backward into a tub of hydrangea. I immediately began scouring the garden in a huff, searching for some sort of plant catastrophe and wondering whether this bill was meant as a replacement cost or a fine. Was I being slapped at financially for failing to display appropriate reverence for all this delicate, intimately imagined greenery? Or punished for Kevin?

I interrogated Mario, deploying my newly acquired ability to speak in the past tense: *"Donde está la planta que fue destruida totalmente??"* Mario professed innocence, *"No se, señora,"* and when I read out the charges brought against me, he shared a sidelong smile, a sign that he agreed that Fernando was being a snob and a goof. Mario allowed that while Geoffrey did tend to shear off the tops of certain plants and pour coffee on others, and while Clara was fond of sprinkling flower petals into the lily pond, as far as Mario could tell, everything was at least still alive.

Vindicated, I planned to storm over to Fernando's *casa* and have it out with him about his preposterous bill for an imaginary calamity, but then I worried that he might retort in various verb tenses that I hadn't yet learned, like the past imperfect or the present imperative, and I wouldn't know what he said.

One day, I found a kitten in my dishwasher. I discovered her after trying to figure out where the meowing sound was coming from in our kitchen, a problem that vexed us for a good eight hours. When we narrowed it down and finally freed her, she scrammed out of the room and shot across our lawn.

The next day she got herself stuck on a ledge somehow, up inside one of the chimneys. More sleuthing, followed by pity and a dish of milk.

Then she couldn't get down from our plum tree. Ambrose refused to come to her rescue again, so I dragged a chair over and clambered up, climbing a tree for the first time in years. The black kitty eyed me curiously and timidly for a time, and then began to purr, rubbing her neck and head against the bark. It struck me that she was engaging in ploys for attention. I don't know anything about cats, but I figure if you're the size of a pine cone and living alone in rural Mexico surrounded by starved dogs and vultures, you probably court attention. At any rate, I could hardly transport her down the tree with both hands without falling myself, so I sent Clara running dutifully and excitedly back to the fed-up Ambrose.

"Daddy, you have to come!" I heard her declare. "Now Mommy is stuck in the tree. Our own MOTHER!"

This is how it goes, creatures big and small blowing through our house, bees the size of trucks banging against the window, coatis taking bites out of the bread, geckos getting caught in the barbecue, spiders in the bathtub, fleas on the kitten, lice in the children's hair, stray dogs of all sizes scuttling under Fernando's flimsy gates and doing cannonballs into the swimming pool. You lose your fear of the creatures after a while and soon simply tend to their needs.

By the time another feral cat gave birth to a litter of four kittens in the shower stall of the guest bathroom, it was nearing the end of our sojourn in Mexico, and I no longer cared about Philip and Fernando and their vision of fine living. They had drawn the wrong lessons from the landscape surrounding them, I had come to decide. They were aspiring to beautify and control nature the way that we more northern North Americans had been doing so obsessively, with so many products to assist us, and for what? We dress our dogs in booties and scoop up their poop, blow-dry their fur, read their minds, and don't give a rat's ass that thousands upon thousands of their southern kin are emaciated and struggling for bare survival.

In the inestimable words of the South African novelist J. M. Coetzee, you look into the eyes of one of these animals, the rudely abandoned offspring of man's "best friend," and flinch at the plea, the profound, incontestable rebuke in their rheumy hopeful faces: "We are too menny."

So, a bid for serenity turns into an incontestable mission that neither therapist nor queen need assign. When you escape a commercial environment that aggressively lays court to the idea that it's all about you, you realize quite succinctly that it is not about you, except insofar as you have the resources, the affluence, and the education to be of help.

In our last weeks in Mexico, I quit my newspaper column in Canada, stopped following the news, and turned my full attention to the ground beneath my feet. We had several stray dogs vaccinated and found homes for three cats, which in Mexico was no easy feat, given their pathetic abundance. We handed most of our possessions to Abondia and Mario and their children, and made preparations to bring three more cats home with us on the plane. We donated money, we sponsored a foster child, and I taught Clara to make fun of a commercial we saw, in which a group of fashion-conscious Barbies chirp: "We live to go shopping!"

Ambrose resold the Chrysler Shadow, which in Toronto would have been rejected as worthless, for God forbid anyone should restore a car that can be tossed and replaced. But he found a man with a cement sofa, whose small child traipsed through the living room during the sale with a dead lizard attached to a string. And this man understood that you don't just toss cars out because they've lost their novelty value and their mufflers. You don't just keep gobbling up the world like greedy freaks with no sense of tomorrow.

A final night in Tepoztlán. The rainy season crashes down upon us now; it pours and thunders and shakes the very walls of our house, sending Kevin to tremble under the bed. Each morning the pool is full of drowned spiders and scorpions and worms, grasshoppers and flying ants and walking sticks and beetles. Flooded carnage. What Geoffrey once threw in that so mortified me is nothing compared to what nature can clog drains with. Who knew? There are moths with fur, and fireflies and mosquitoes and millipedes as long as my foot. The rain is a deluge, a wondrous, theatrical cleansing that makes a mockery of control.

As I write a final journal entry, a daddy-long-legs soft-shoes down the wall beside me, and the cicadas and crickets keep up their continuous chorus. Our phone is out again and the car is broken down. I had to gather up Geoffrey and Clara and their end-of-school artwork, just abandon the car for its new owner to fetch and repair, marching my youngsters up the cobblestone street to one of the town's main thoroughfares in order to catch a taxi, whose driver I now knew by name.

We left two kittens behind at the school in a *canasta*; one went home with the cook, the other with a little girl in *primera*. I wonder how they will fare, the bewildered little sweeties, and where they will sleep. The other three will, at least, have one another and us, as they undertake their strange adventure on Aero Mexico and land in a world of unimaginable animal luxury.

Funny. This final night. The stress of our departure is almost non-existent compared with our arrival. No racing mind; no irritability or anxiety. Suitcases packed, and whatever happens happens. Striking. I have genuinely slowed myself down, looked around me, grown purposeful and thus relaxed.

Mañana, mañana, as the Mexicans say. Every day has its essential tasks.

ACKNOWLEDGEMENTS

Heartfelt thanks to the following people, for their mentorship and faith:

Dianne deFenoyl, formerly of the *National Post*, for whom many of these pieces were originally written.

Glen Nishimura at *USA Today*, who goads me to keep making sense of the news, in spite of frequent episodes on my part of wretching like a cat.

Patricia Hluchy at *Maclean's*, who was my champion and became my friend.

Anne Collins at Random House Canada, whose loyalty is the highest compliment a writer could be paid. (Thanks also to Kendall, Craig, Marion, Frances.)

Lucia Macro at William Morrow, who took a chance on me, for which I will always be grateful.

Gillian Blake at Bloomsbury USA, who invited me into a house that feels like home.

Paula Balzer and Sarah Lazin, the agents who edit, and manage, and nourish, and provide comfy beds. Without them, frankly: what career?

For inspiration, feedback, love, and laffs thanks to:

Landon, Geoff, Hilary, Katharine, Anne, and Michael Pearson; also Keri, Mark, Doug, Dot & Whay, Patsy, and the Mackenzie and Pearson clans.

To my brilliantly funny friends, whose sly wit would have given the Algonquin Round Table a run for its money, thank you: Kenton Zavits, Ric Bienstock, Michael DeCarlo, Karen Zagor, Eric Reguly, Paula Bowley, Blair Robins, Dave Eddie, Pam Seatle, Pier Bryden, Elaine Evans, Sheila Whyte, Clayton Kennedy, Daphne Ballon, Steve and Jeff Butler, Claire Welland, Shannon Black, Russell Monk, Doug Bell, David Hannah, Bill Rogers, Janet Allon, John Allore, Robert Labossiere, Patrick Graham, and Jessica Macdonald, to name but a few. I've been blessed.

Gratitude to my collaborators at the *National Post*, Natasha Hassan, Theresa Butcher, Sheila McKevenue, Dianna Symonds, and Gerald Owen in particular.

Muchos abrazos, también, a mis amigos en Mexico, incluyendo mi madrina, Margaret Del Rio; Arturo Marquez; Sylvia; y Pip.

And finally, to my little pack, with whom I trundle hither and yon across the landscape, generally making a mess: Clara, Geoffrey, and Ambrose, with a special hug to Nanny Verdlyn.

A NOTE ON THE AUTHOR

Patricia Pearson is a frequent contributor to *USA Today* and the author of the novels *Playing House* and *Believe Me*. Her work has appeared in the *New York Times*, the *New York Observer*, the *Guardian*, and *Redbook*, among other publications. She has won three Canadian National Magazine Awards, as well as an Arthur Ellis Award (Best Non-fiction Crime Book) for *When She Was Bad*. As well, *Playing House* was nominated for the Stephen Leacock Memorial Medal for Humour. She recently moved from Toronto to the boreal forest outside Montreal with her husband and two children.